MAGITECH SOARS

MAGITECH SOARS

EXCEPTIONAL SOPHIA BEAUFONT™ BOOK 06

SARAH NOFFKE
MICHAEL ANDERLE

DISRUPTIVE IMAGINATION

LMBPN Publishing
PMB 196, 2540 South Maryland Pkwy
Las Vegas, NV 89109

Version 1.00, November 2021
(Previously published as a part of the megabook *Magitech Rises)*
eBook ISBN: 978-1-68500-594-8
Print ISBN: 978-1-68500-595-5

THE MAGITECH SOARS TEAM

Thanks to the JIT Readers

Angel LaVey
Billie Leigh Kellar
Dave Hicks
Deb Mader
Debi Sateren
Diane L. Smith
Dorothy Lloyd
Jackey Hankard-Brodie
Jeff Eaton
Jeff Goode
Kathleen Fettig
Larry Omans
Lori Hendricks
Micky Cocker
Misty Roa
Nicole Emens
Paul Westman
Peter Manis
Veronica Stephan-Miller

If we've missed anyone, please let us know!

Editor
The Skyhunter Editing Team

Once again and a thousand times more, for Lydia.

— Sarah

*To Family, Friends and
Those Who Love
to Read.
May We All Enjoy Grace
to Live the Life We Are
Called.*

— Michael

.

CHAPTER ONE

Over four hundred and fifty years ago

Having ripped the fabric of his cloak into pieces, Hiker Wallace worked fast, knowing he was losing blood quickly. Without the warmth of his cape, the chill of the Highland air made his teeth chatter, but it was more important to stop the bleeding from the knife wound in his leg than stay warm.

The blade had hit an artery, based on how much it was bleeding. The magician was too light-headed to use magic to seal the wound. Even if Hiker could use magic, he wasn't competent enough with healing spells to ensure it wouldn't backfire. His quiet life, traveling across the highlands and looking for meaning, hadn't offered Hiker many opportunities to learn different branches of magic.

In his forty years on Earth, Hiker had run across few people during his travels. It had been a surprise to him to find the one person he'd been trying to avoid most of his life in the middle of nowhere.

"Hiker!" Thad Reinhart yelled. His voice echoed over the

green hills and carried across the loch in the distance. "Come out, come out, wherever you are!"

Hiker tensed behind the boulder where he was hiding. His twin brother sounded close, and why wouldn't he be? Of course, Thad had gained on him. Thad could run much faster than Hiker, always the more agile one, and with the leg wound, he had a considerable advantage.

"You know, I've been trying to find you for over two decades!" Thad yelled, his Scottish accent thicker than Hiker's due to his lack of education. His voice sounded almost giddy with excitement. "You do know that, don't you? You bloody coward. You've been running for way too long."

Ever since Thad found out if one twin died, the other would inherit their magical power he'd been trying to murder Hiker. It had simply been an extra motivation. Thad had been trying to kill Hiker since the beginning. His nature was to take out anyone who had more than him—anyone he considered had wronged him, even if inadvertently.

Hiker's mistake had been in just existing. No matter what he tried to do, his twin brother would never accept him. And magic made it all the worse.

Hiker tied another bit of his torn cloak around his wound and tried to breathe through his mouth as the searing pain nearly made him pass out. He pulled the shredded cloak back over his shoulders, careful to stay low.

It was only a matter of time before Thad found him in his hiding spot. Hiker should have realized it was only a matter of time before his twin found him in general. He knew their connection gave them hints about the other. Often he saw flashes of Thad's life—the people he swindled, the treasures he'd stolen, the ones he abused...killed.

Living in the highlands had made it easier for Hiker to shield his thoughts from his brother. Time had helped too. But it hadn't lasted, and now Thad had found him and would finish him for good.

"You gave it all up for this!" Thad yelled, his voice closer. Hiker pictured him sweeping his arms wide at the vast rolling hills all around them. "You had the riches I deserved. The parents I should have had. The life meant for me. And you gave it all up because you were scared, knowing if you stuck around, I'd kill you, you bloody coward."

Hiker heard his brother spit and assumed Thad was wearing a look of disgust.

He couldn't argue with a word he said because Thad was right. Hiker had run, had given up his family's legacy, his inheritance, and a prosperous life. But what had he been supposed to do? It was kill Thad or be killed by him. There was no other way.

He'd even offered to split the inheritance, but his twin wouldn't go for it. Thad had contended he should have had it all from the beginning.

The twin's parents had both died when they were infants, forcing the children to be separated shortly after birth. Hiker had been sent to live with his father's parents, an affluent family who owned a lucrative business and were considered very respectable. The Wallace's were loving people who gave Hiker many opportunities to learn and succeed. They sent him to the best schools and gave him the very best of everything. They even made efforts for Hiker to spend time with his twin, who lived on the far side of town.

Thad went to live with their mother's family—the Reinharts. They lived in squalor and were considered criminals by most. Thad was often abused or neglected, but any time the Wallace family tried to get him away, they were fought. The patriarch of the Reinhart family, an angry drunk, argued Thad was the last he had of his daughter, and he wouldn't let him go. He didn't really want the boy. Mostly he just wanted another thief in his charge.

He wanted someone he could abuse and control. Someone who could help run his scams and do his bidding.

The boys grew up living very different lives. Thad had never forgiven Hiker for the life he considered so much better than his.

One might contend it was circumstances which made Hiker the good-hearted man and Thad rotten to the core, but like attracts like. When the boys were divided up shortly after birth, the good twin was magnetized to the healthy home, and the bad one sent with people more like him.

Thad's heart had been blackened from the beginning. Hiker later learned that much when he researched connections between twins, trying to shield his brother from finding him. That had been shortly after it came to light that when one twin died, the other inherited their magical power.

What neither twin knew was, destiny had dictated their path from the beginning. Thad had been born bad, and Hiker, good. It was set up that way for a reason. The angels had seen to it. Balance in the world was important, and these two men were a part of that. Soon, they'd meet their matches.

All twins destined to ride dragons fulfilled a certain destiny. One was always good. The other was purely bad. There was no escaping it. Only the angels and Mother Nature knew the true reason for this.

These two men knew they were twins but no more because their true destiny hadn't found them—but it was about to.

"You know," Thad said, his voice no longer booming. He was dangerously close. "I should have killed you when I had the chance. When we were in the womb. All I would have had to do was wrap my umbilical cord around your neck, and none of this would have been an issue. Alas, I did not and now..."

The cold wind stroked Hiker's face; almost a comforting thing, he thought. It was followed by the opposite as his twin rose over him, standing on the boulder where he was shielding himself.

Hiker stiffened.

It had all come down to this.

There was no escaping. He knew that much. The expansive hills offered many paths for escape, but none were available to Hiker in his current condition. He wouldn't get ten yards before his brother struck him down and killed him for good.

He wanted to close his eyes and not watch as Thad pulled a sword from his belt, a greedy look on his face, but he wouldn't allow himself to look away. Although Hiker had run all these years, it hadn't been to avoid his own death. It had been to avoid his brother's. There was no reality where he could fight Thad and kill him, and that was the only option as far as his twin was concerned. Ironically he'd now die by Thad's hands because he was unwilling to fight him.

Hiker Wallace was anything but a coward. He simply didn't have what it took to keep fighting someone he wanted to love. His heart, time and time again, failed to understand why Thad wanted power when love was the better option. Why Thad hurt others when peace could heal him. There was so much Hiker didn't understand about his twin.

When Thad stood on the boulder above Hiker, he forgot it all and tried to make amends with the man who had haunted him all his life.

"I'm sorry," Hiker said, looking straight up into his brother's eyes as he stood above him, making him crane his neck. "I'm sorry you don't want me alive. I'm sorry you had to live with the Reinharts. But more than anything, I'm sorry you'd rather have my power than the life we could have had together."

A cold chuckle lacking all humor spilled from Thad's mouth. He was poised, ready to jump down in front of his brother and deliver the blow he'd dreamed of for so long—the one that finished Hiker. But, as was Thad's style, he was going to relish the moment.

"I never wanted you as my twin or my brother," Thad said

through clenched teeth. "Why share this world with the inept when I can rule it alone!"

Hiker saw the telegraphed moves that signaled what his brother would do next. It was the flexing of his muscles. The arching of his back. The glint in his eyes. Hiker knew he wouldn't be able to escape the next series of actions.

When Thad jumped off the boulder, sword in hand, Hiker was astounded by what happened next.

A large shimmering red *something* shot across his vision. It happened so fast he only caught a glimpse as it knocked Thad off the rock and launched him several dozen yards, where he landed in the grass and rolled down the hill, far away.

Hiker had never seen a beast like the one that landed right after Thad was thrown. His brother continued to roll head over feet as Hiker tried to stand, one hand on his injured leg and one hand on his weapon.

Upon getting to his feet, he surprised himself by dropping his sword and letting it fall to the grass. He only caught a brief glimpse of Thad as he recovered. He looked up with shock as the great magical creature unfurled her wings before tucking them into her massive body, covered in sparkling scales.

The good twin had never seen a dragon. He thought they were just lore. As he looked into the ancient eyes of the dragon whose name he knew by heart, for no apparent reason, he knew dragons were real—and this one, somehow, someway, belonged to him.

With his remaining strength, before the pain in his heart and his leg made him sleep, Hiker sunk into a low bow and showed his respect to the dragon.

"It is a pleasure to meet you, Bell," he said when he rose, not at all understanding what was happening, but embracing it at once. He had no clue how he knew the dragon's name or knew her at all, but like magnets, he felt the draw.

The dragon lowered her massive head, her eyes shimmering with acceptance for the magician before her.

We've always known each other, Hiker Wallace, she replied. *But only now can our lives together commence as they were always meant to.*

Thad Reinhart watched from the bottom of the hill, his eyes burning with hatred. Not only had he failed to kill the one man he'd wanted dead for so long, but now Hiker had something else he wanted.

He turned and sped for the mountains, intent on finding another way to end his brother.

Little did he know, waiting for him by the stream where he'd seek refreshment, was his own dragon.

And like him, Ember's heart was black.

Like Thad, she'd been born that way.

CHAPTER TWO

"Whose balls are freezing right now?" Evan asked, his teeth chattering.

"This shouldn't come as a surprise to you, but not mine," Sophia answered as she pressed her hands deeper into her wool-lined pockets.

"My balls aren't freezing either," Ainsley said, striding out of the Castle carrying a tray with glasses of whisky.

"Why do we have to do this?" Evan complained and squinted in Hiker's direction.

All of the riders, Ainsley, and Quiet, were gathered in front of the Castle, the only light came from the stars in the darkened sky and the flames burning in the windows. All of the electrical lights, which the Castle had started to include in different areas, especially for the Christmas decorations, had been extinguished for the countdown. Hiker wasn't a fan of the growing trend of electric items being included in the Castle, but Sophia was confident he'd come around in time.

"First-footing is a tradition," Hiker explained. "And since Sophia is making us celebrate holidays—"

"Making?" she interrupted. "I refuse to apologize for bringing a bit of cheer to this place."

"Yes, but you should apologize for the five pounds I've put on eating holiday sweets," Ainsley said, handing a glass to each person.

"You're a shapeshifter," Wilder said, taking the whisky. "Can't you just shift to a form where you are five pounds lighter?"

"I can, but then I'm not my authentic self," Ainsley said self-righteously, lifting her nose.

"You once spent an entire year in the form of a giant," Evan pointed out.

"It was only because I was mad at the Castle and wanted to wear out the furnishings faster with my larger form," Ainsley explained.

"If you all are quite done, it's almost time for Hogmanay," Hiker said, holding up his glass of whisky and queuing the others to join him in a toast.

Hogmanay was the Scottish word for New Year's eve and came with its own traditions. They were all new to Sophia, except for the idea of toasting with a nice drink after the countdown.

For this occasion, Hiker had broken out a very old bottle of whisky but grumbled about it. Sophia knew better, though. He was coming around, and it had all started with his confession to her about being Thad Reinhart's twin.

His office was back to normal, but she suspected the Castle was still finding ways to annoy him. Not because he was keeping a secret but rather just because the sentient building liked to be entertained.

Eyeing his watch, Hiker began, "The New Year starts in five, four, three, two, one."

When the countdown was over, everyone cheered, "Happy New Year."

Sophia clinked her glass with the others before taking a sip.

Her insides were instantly warmed from the whisky, which could make her start sweating if she drank enough of it, although it was bitterly cold on the Expanse.

"You're not making us link arms and sing Auld Lang Syne, are you?" Ainsley asked the leader of the Dragon Elite.

"I don't think anyone wants to hear you sing," Evan said, finishing his drink and holding it out to the shapeshifter. "I'd like more."

"And I'd like you to have manners, alas that reality is not happening, just like your refill," Ainsley stated and poked her tongue out at the dragonrider.

"Fine, I'll get it myself." Evan stalked for the Castle door.

"No, you won't." Hiker reached out and held Evan back by the shoulder. "First footing."

Evan cast him a backward glance. "Yes, and you said that means a tall, dark, and handsome man has to be the first one to enter the 'house' at the start of the New Year. That's me."

"Why can't it be a female?" Sophia asked.

Hiker regarded her with mild irritation. "Because that's considered unlucky."

She rolled her eyes. "I swear, if the Dragon Elite had a human resource department, I'd lodge a complaint."

He blinked at her and returned her challenging expression. "But we don't, so get over it."

"I think it should be Mahkah who does the first footing because he's nicer than the lot of you," Ainsley said, smiling at the quiet dragonrider still nursing his drink.

"Thank you," he said and blushed.

Quiet muttered something as he strode out to the grounds, his drink in hand as he sauntered away.

"Oh, Quiet, I would have picked you, but you aren't what we'd call tall," Ainsley called after the gnome, who was still muttering and obviously agitated.

"It's going to be Wilder," Hiker declared. He pointed at the door, his eyes on the dragonrider standing next to Sophia.

"Why does he get to do it?" Evan complained.

"Because I drew straws, and his was the one I picked," Hiker said definitively.

Ainsley elbowed Mahkah in the side and whispered loudly, "I think it's because he's got a man-crush on him."

Wilder tilted his head to the side as he ran his fingers through his brown hair and smiled. "Why, thank you. I'd be happy to do the first footing. I am tall, dark and—"

"Full of yourself," Evan interrupted.

"You're one to talk," Sophia said.

"What are you all doing out here?" Mama Jamba called at their back as she hurried across the icy grounds toward the Castle.

Hiker blinked at her in confusion. "What are you doing out here? Where have you been?"

She smiled up at the large man. She looked small in comparison. "Papa Creola and I have a long-standing tradition on the New Year. He winds the clock, and then we—"

"Kiss!" Evan exclaimed, laughing.

"Show some respect," Hiker scolded.

"Oh, no, he's absolutely right," Mama Jamba said with a giggle. "We smooch at the start of the New Year."

"You do?" Sophia asked, trying to picture the hippie elf kissing Mama Jamba.

She nodded. "Yes. We missed one year, and the consequences were far-reaching." She leaned forward and in a conspiratorial whisper said, "That was the year Pepsi Cola was invented. We're still trying to fix the ramifications to come out of that."

"Like childhood obesity?" Sophia asked.

"Like there are certain venues which only carry Pepsi products," Mama Jamba answered. "What are you all doing out here freezing your tails off?"

"Balls," Evan corrected.

"You watch your mouth in front of Mama," Hiker admonished before turning his attention back to Mother Nature. "We were just about to do the first-footing."

"Oh!" she cheered. "I love that you're being so festive this year." With a smile, Mama Jamba pointed to the front door of the Castle. "Go on then, Wilder. Go on through."

"What?" Evan threw his hands up. "Why Wilder?"

Mama Jamba leveled her gaze on him. "Because his straw got pulled, obviously."

"Yeah, obviously," Wilder said and headed for the front door.

Sophia shuffled forward, following the group as Wilder stepped over the threshold. "Thanks for allowing this," she said to Hiker in a low voice.

His gaze shifted to her, his face expressionless. "Well, I guess it was overdue."

"And thanks for the cookie bouquet you got me for Christmas," she said.

His brow wrinkled. "What are you talking about? I didn't get you a cookie bouquet."

She nodded. "No, no, you didn't. But since you asked, my birthday is in the summer, and I'd totally love a cookie bouquet."

"What's a cookie bouquet?" Hiker asked.

"Pretty much exactly what it sounds like," she answered, enjoying the warmth of the Castle as she entered.

"And where do I get these cookie bouquets?" he questioned.

Sophia's face transformed with shock. "Are you really going to get me one for my birthday? I can get you some names of companies who make them."

Hiker shook his head. "No, one of my next projects as a world adjudicator will be to dismantle all companies who make cookie bouquets."

She scowled at him. "Ha-ha."

"Sophia," Mama Jamba called from the staircase, pointing at

the second floor. "I want you in bed right away. You have training early tomorrow morning."

"But there's more whisky," Ainsley said, holding up a bottle of amber-colored liquid.

"Mama says Sophia is going to bed, so that's what she's doing," Hiker ordered. He also held up a hand and pointed to the second floor.

Sophia couldn't help but smile as she trudged for the stairs. "Yes, Mom and Dad."

At the base of the stairs, Mama Jamba leaned forward and planted a kiss on Sophia's cheek. "Happy New Year, dear. Please rest up since this will be your biggest year yet. Well, until the next one, if we make it past this one."

"On that somber note," Wilder said, "sleep tight, Soph. Dream good dreams, and don't worry about the Earth ending."

Sophia smirked. "Yeah, I'm sure I'll drift right off to sleep after this."

CHAPTER THREE

A peaceful wind rolled across the Expanse as Sophia and Mahkah strode out toward the Cave the next morning. Everyone in the Castle was still sleeping after the late night of celebrating. It had been difficult for Sophia to fall asleep, but not because she was worried about her training or the future. There was that, but mostly it was because Evan kept yelling things from the first-floor like, "I'm tall!" "I'm handsome!" "I'm the darkest one here!"

The icy grass crunched under their boots as they moved in the direction of the dragons lounging in the morning sun on the Expanse.

"Do you have everything you need?" Mahkah asked her.

She patted her sides. "The clothes on my back, my sword, and a whole lot of hope. I have everything I'm allowed, but not sure about need. I could use a bag of Doritos for the trip."

He released a small smile. "I get you're not allowed a lot for such a long and arduous task, but it's the only way."

When Mahkah told Sophia her next training with Lunis was to venture out into the middle of nowhere with no supplies and survive for a week on their own, she wasn't excited. They couldn't use magic to survive in the Australian Outback. Instead, they had to rely on each other to find water, food, and shelter.

Similar to a walkabout, this training exercise was supposed to be reflective for the pair, to help them to know their inner selves. It was also apparently going to bring them closer or drive them apart. The way they came out of the experience was crucial to whether they passed or not.

Not only did Sophia not want to sleep in a place with some of the most dangerous animals in the world without magic, but she was sad to leave the Castle. It felt like a strange thing to do on the first day of the New Year. However, Mama Jamba had been adamant Sophia throw herself into training, and this was apparently one of the hardest tasks to complete. If she got through the walkabout with Lunis, hopefully the rest of their training would be considerably easier.

Lunis was rolling around in the grass like a dog after a bath when they approached. The other dragons were eyeing him with obvious speculation. It seemed to Sophia, the stranger the other dragons found Lunis the more it encouraged his odd behavior. At first, he'd worried about being so different from the others, having been raised at a different time with different influences, but now he seemed to embrace it.

The blue dragon rolled onto his feet and ran over when Sophia was near. Affectionately she glanced up at the majestic dragon. She sensed he was extra playful this morning, trying to put her fears at ease with his light nature.

For someone who hadn't gone a day without magic since she was a toddler, it was bizarre to Sophia to consider not using it for a week. Even weirder was the idea of feeding herself when she'd always had such things provided for her. But that was the point in the training exercise, and although Lunis wasn't going to allow her to starve, Sophia knew she had to learn how to fend for herself. A dragon's job wasn't to support their rider. It was to be a part of an equal partnership.

Are you ready for this? Lunis asked her, his tone enthusiastic.

"Of course," she said, trying to inject excitement into her voice.

While Lunis is gone, Coral remarked, *who is going to make an exorbitant amount of noise in the Cave and go on for hours about who is winning on the Disguise?*

The show is called the Mask, Lunis corrected. *And you will just have to survive without me. I'm certain you'll be bored to death within a day or two.*

The purple dragon scowled at him, impassively batting her eyes. *And yet somehow, we've survived for hundreds of years without your nonsense.*

Hundreds of long, boring years, Lunis stated. *You're going to miss me. Just you wait.*

Coral shook her head and took off, rising high in the sky and circling around before heading for the flock of sheep on the Eastern hills.

"Don't eat the agnostic ones," Sophia called after the dragon. "Their indecision will give you a stomachache."

Lunis cringed. *Oh no, you didn't.*

"What?" Sophia complained. "Mama Jamba said the sheep have religious affiliations. You're talking to ancient dragons about reality television, but I make a joke about agnostics, and that's too much?"

I think Mama Jamba was pulling your leg, Lunis offered. *I don't think sheep are religious.*

"Why, because they aren't educated on such things?" Sophia asked.

He shook his head. *Because they tend to be more scientifically-minded.*

Sophia laughed. "You're so ridiculous. I can't believe I'm even having this conversation with you."

"To be honest," Mahkah cut in, stepping up beside Sophia. "I can't believe I'm listening to this discussion between a dragon and a rider."

Sophia offered him a wink. "We are a unique pair."

"Indeed, you are," he agreed, bowing respectfully. "And I look forward to you both returning. Things won't be the same here without you. You might have noticed I tend to be of a more serious nature."

Get out of town, Lunis said with mock surprise.

Mahkah flashed a subtle smile. "Having you two around is good for us. I've often thought the older dragonriders took themselves too seriously, and you help to liven things up."

"I will admit my impression has been the same," Sophia stated. "Dragonriders do seem serious."

That's because crusty old men, set in their ways, get crotchety, Lunis stated.

"I won't argue with that," Mahkah said, not at all offended by this observation. "Your perspective is refreshing."

"Thank you," Sophia said, returning the slight bow.

"Now, just one more thing before you leave." Mahkah held out his hand.

Without missing a beat, Sophia slapped his palm like he was offering her a high-five.

He shook his head. "No, I think you know what I want."

She sighed and rolled her eyes as she fished into her pocket. Of course, Mahkah knew she'd been trying to smuggle her phone on the trip. She withdrew the iPhone and handed it over. "I was just going to take it so I could chronicle our experiences and later blog about it."

"I don't know what blog is, but you know the rules," Mahkah instructed.

She nodded. "Yes, no electronics, magic, or contact with any outsiders."

"That's right," he affirmed. "Any of those things will end your training, and you'll have to restart it from the beginning."

"One week," Sophia stated, chewing on her lip. It seemed like a long time to go without her phone or magic, but more than anything, her friends. She could hardly believe how much she'd grown accustomed to having the other dragonriders, Ainsley, and Quiet around.

She was grateful she'd have her best friend. That would get her through. Even if she didn't know how to purify water or hunt or anything else, she had Lunis, and that was what mattered most.

CHAPTER FOUR

The last bit of magic Sophia and Lunis could use for a whole week was to create and close the portal into the Australian Outback. Technically, dragons flew by way of magic, but that was apparently permissible.

"Seems like there are some loopholes to this magic using business," Sophia mused as they flew toward the mostly flat red earth sprinkled with vegetation. Mountains framed the area, and a stream ran through the hills.

I wouldn't advise pushing any boundaries on this, Lunis said as he landed. *If you break a rule and we end up here longer, we're going to have words.*

Sophia laughed. "You just don't want to miss the Super Bowl."

Don't be ridiculous, he replied. *That's in February. There's no way we'll be out here that long. But going longer than I have to without Netflix and frozen yogurt isn't advisable for my overall morale.*

"It's a good thing you were born in the twenty-first century," she offered. "Could you imagine being born when Bell was?"

He sighed and shook out his wings before folding them elegantly beside his body. *No. Did you know she has never had frozen yogurt?*

Unsurprisingly, it was hot in the Australian Outback. Sophia peeled off her cloak and tied it around her waist. "I'm certain you're the only dragon ever to have frozen yogurt."

The Outback was what Sophia had expected. Miles and miles of trees, bush, mountains, and, she suspected, creepy, crawly creatures waiting to attack her in the night.

"So, first things first," she said, surveying the area.

Where's the Starbucks? Lunis asked.

Sophia pointed. "I think it's on the other side of the ridge."

Cool, I'll race you.

"Lun, I'll never win that race, so no."

He nodded and ran his long claws through the dirt. Observing how it moved told him something about this place. *I think our first order of business should be to find shelter.*

Shielding her eyes, Sophia looked out at the desert before them. "Maybe we should set up camp beside that bush, or that one." She indicated the two areas. "I don't know, which bush do you think has the fewest scorpions who will want to crawl into my pants?"

Hard to say, he muttered, considering the question. *I think we'll want to be close to a water source and have the shade of the mountains.*

Sophia gazed at where the closest water source was, according to her earlier dragon's-eye view. It was at least a five-mile trek. She wished they had planned better and landed by the river rather than in their current location. Mahkah had instructed her to land right after going through the portal. He was very serious about them not using magic, and although Lunis could fly, she wasn't supposed to ride him until the week was up.

Sophia wasn't sure how Mahkah or Hiker would know if she broke the rules, but something told her they had their methods.

"Okay, let's hoof it," Sophia said, starting toward the river.

Cool, Lunis chirped. He unfurled his wings and instantly received a punishing glare from Sophia. *Oh, so now you don't want me flying because you have to walk?*

"It doesn't seem fair," she retorted. "Aren't we supposed to be together anyway? Bonding."

Fine, he surrendered. *I'll walk with you, but if we see a snake, I'm air-bound.*

"You've got to be kidding me!" Sophia exclaimed. "You're a freaking dragon."

Have you seen *snakes?* Lunis argued. *I'm still human...I mean, vulnerable. I have feelings, you know. I'm allowed to have fears.*

"Is this when we start bonding, discussing all our memories and whatnot?" Sophia asked.

Sure, Lunis began, ambling beside her, moving slower than he had to keep pace. *Why don't you share some of your fears with me?*

"Well..." Sophia thought for a moment. "I used to be afraid of the dark but—"

But now you love it because you know there's more to fear in the light than otherwise, Lunis interrupted.

She nodded. "Yeah, I guess you have access to my thoughts."

Are there other fears I don't know about? Lunis asked.

"Well, I worry about you and I being successful. A lot is resting on our shoulders, and—"

Of course, you always worry about Liv in her role as Warrior for the House of Fourteen and Clark finding happiness since he's prone to being overly anxious, Lunis cut in again.

Sophia slumped. "Is there anything you don't know about me?"

He shook his head. *Sometimes you say something I know you're going to say, but you say it in a way I wasn't expecting.*

She sighed. "Well, how about you? Tell me something about you I didn't know, like that you're afraid of snakes."

I'm really not, he confessed. *I just said that to make you laugh.*

"It worked," she affirmed.

Okay, about me... Lunis thought for a moment. *Well, when I hatched—*

"I was there," Sophia interrupted.

Right, he growled. *Well, let's see, my favorite flavor of fro-yo is—*

"Cookies and cream," she cut in. "You think you're allergic to honey, but you have no scientific evidence to back that up."

Because you won't take me to a doctor! the dragon complained.

Sophia shook her head, ignoring his outburst. "You can read but not phonetically, which is why you mispronounce words so often. You're a Virgo, which means you think you know everything. You say your favorite show is *Nailed it* on Netflix, but it's actually *Doctor Who* on BBC. You wish you were all Hollywood, but you're really all nerdy. And Taylor Swift is your spirit animal."

Lunis halted and gave her a perturbed expression. *First off, reading is hard.*

"You were born with the skill," Sophia pointed out. "Try having to learn on your own without the collective chi of the dragon to be able to do things."

Sounds hard, Lunis said unsympathetically. *No, thanks. And I like* Nailed It, *but how can I not be a fan of David Tennant? He's so dreamy.*

"You're so weird," Sophia laughed.

And I'm not apologizing for Tay-Tay, Lunis stated. *She's a real American diva. I think we should get tickets for the next show.*

"Why not just fly in and sit on the top of the amphitheater?" Sophia suggested.

Because I want access to the concessions, Lunis argued. *Maybe we get a private box?*

"Maybe…" Sophia's voice trailed away as she tried to think of something Lunis didn't know about her or something she didn't know about him and could ask.

"I don't think there's anything we don't know about each other," she finally said.

"I was going to mention that," he offered. *So a week together? This won't get boring.*

Sophia shrugged. "It's like we're alone with ourselves because you are, in essence, me and I'm you. It would make sense there would be a little less conversation and a lot more introspection."

This is when we start contemplating our navels, he said.

"You don't have a navel," she corrected.

I know, but you do, so I can live vicariously through you.

"I hope that's not going to work in all situations," Sophia muttered.

Well, I feel like I know what it's like to have a uterus, he shared.

"Gross," Sophia shot back at him.

Do you feel like you know what it's like to breathe fire? he asked.

"No, not at all," she answered.

Oh, well, then, you might want to work on your connection to me, he suggested. *Maybe if you connect to me during this walkabout, you'll feel the chi of the dragon more.*

"First, we have to walk about five miles." She pointed to the mountains in the distance.

Lunis shook his head. *Can I request no more puns for the week?*

"You can, but I can't guarantee it," Sophia replied.

After a long silence of kicking up red dirt and nothing else, Lunis huffed. *Soooooo…*

"Yeah, sooooo," Sophia replied.

Do you sort of feel like an old married couple? he asked.

"Yeah, and it didn't take us that long to get there," she replied.

Do you miss the guys?

"Maybe. Actually, strangely, yes," she admitted.

I miss the other dragons.

"Well, I don't miss Evan yet, so that's a good sign."

I'm sure we'll figure it out, Lunis said. *This week is supposed to bond us.*

"Or make us hate each other," Sophia offered.

Yeah, I'm sure seven days in extreme heat and horrible living conditions with zero chance of frozen yogurt won't do that for us.

Sophia looked meaningfully at her dragon. "Please, and I ask this from the bottom of my heart. Please don't eat me this week."

He nodded. *I will try. You try not to use bad puns, and hopefully, we will meet in the middle.*

CHAPTER FIVE

By the time Sophia made it to the river, she was starving. She'd been too nervous about the walkabout that morning to eat breakfast, which was now backfiring on her.

"So, we have to feed ourselves." Sophia looked around at the dry vegetation.

"That's going to be harder for some of us than others," Lunis said, his gaze drifting to a mob of kangaroos traveling across the bush in the distance. They were quite a distance away, but the chi of the dragon made it so the pair could easily spot them. Lunis gave the mob a hungry glare before giving Sophia a questioning expression.

"Oh, fine." She waved him off. "Go on then. Go get a kangaroo. I'll gather some berries or something."

"Don't eat anything blue," he suggested. "That's age-old wisdom."

"What about blueberries?" she asked.

"That's the exception," he stated.

"How about a blue dragon?" she continued to ask.

He shook his head. "Whatever you do, don't eat a blue dragon. Bad stomach aches will result in serious cramps."

She shrugged. "Doesn't sound worse than when I eat nachos from Taco Bell."

"May I suggest," he began, "not eating nachos from Taco Bell."

"You can," she offered. "But I reserve the right to ignore such bad advice."

"Okay, so I'm going to go hunt a kangaroo," Lunis said, his eyes hungry as he regarded the mob in the distance.

"And I'm going to find a platter of nachos somewhere in the near vicinity," Sophia said, looking around speculatively.

Lunis glanced at the area, a skeptical glare in his eyes. "Yeah, good luck with that. If you don't find any, I'll share my kangaroo with you."

Sophia shook her head. "No, but thank you. I'm catching my own dinner, and then we will set up camp."

"And collect water," Lunis reminded her.

Sophia sighed. "This whole thing is a lot of work."

He nodded. "It's a full-time job. Just wait. You'll see."

It seemed more like a threat rather than a promise, Sophia mused as her dragon flew off into the clear blue sky, leaving her to fend for herself.

CHAPTER SIX

Sophia kicked around the dirt by the tree she was stationed by and considered her options.

"This is not such a big deal," she said to herself, realizing she had already started to lose her mind if she was talking to herself in the Outback. *Sooner rather than later,* she thought. "All I need to do is find dinner. No biggie. People have been doing it since the beginning of time."

The sun was still high in the sky, and Lunis looked close to selecting his entrée for dinner. She had a sword and could go and slaughter a beast, but that would mean traveling. She'd already crossed many miles across the Outback and felt as hot as a furnace, the heat really starting to register for her.

"It would be better if dinner came to me," she mused, thinking of Uber Eats, but knowing it wasn't an option.

A scratching noise from under the base of the tree where she was stationed caught her attention.

Sophia turned to the sound. "That seems like dinner is calling."

She crouched down low and stuck her face into the hole next to the tree. It was deep and dark, and she really didn't like the idea of digging in there to draw out prey. What she really wanted was whatever was in there to come out and say "hi" to her. Then she could use Inexorabilis to slice it in half and cook it over a fire.

"Fire," she said, looking around speculatively. "That's right, I need to be able to make fire without magic."

It shouldn't be hard since she'd prepared for this part of the adventure, studying up on ways to make fire. The tree with her dinner under it provided not only the perfect source for fire but also the ideal way to draw her food out.

It was a eucalyptus tree, and its oil was considered extremely flammable. Not only would the flaking bark make great kindling, but the oil would make a great fire starter. Sophia smiled triumphantly. As a bonus, the eucalyptus oil would also make a great bomb—one she'd throw into the burrow to draw out her corned beef and hash, or rodent, or whatever it ended up being.

She hoped it would be corned beef but had serious doubts.

CHAPTER SEVEN

Do you really think that's going to work? Lunis asked.

She pushed the sweat pouring into her eyes away with the back of her hand. *No, I'm just making homemade bombs because I don't think they will work.*

Sarcasm is the scared man's way of keeping others at a distance, Lunis intoned. He was trying to sound sage-like, but a hint of mischief in his voice rang through.

Where did you get that proverb from? Sophia asked.

I made it up, Lunis said. *Dragons are considered very wise, so I was thinking of coming up with a bunch of dragon proverbs. Maybe publish a book of them.*

You need t-shirts, Sophia said, wrapping the soaked eucalyptus leaves in dry twigs like a bird making a strange nest. She'd been playing with figuring out the best design for her homemade bombs. It needed to have a fuse of sorts, and of course, an explosive element, but not so explosive it killed whatever was hiding in the burrow under the tree. She just wanted to scare it out, and then she'd sword it up and serve it on... Sophia looked around. She'd have to serve it on a leaf or something since the Outback was fresh out of plates, it seemed.

I like the way you think, Lunis approved. *T-shirts are a good idea, and we can make a board on Pinterest.*

You're not allowed to use my Pinterest account anymore.

Because I keep filling your boards up with baking recipes, he replied.

Yes, that's exactly right, she answered. *And you don't even bake. I don't get the logistics of how a dragon would bake. Like, can you work a hand mixer?*

He snorted with laughter in her head. *I think you're missing the hint. I don't bake, but I do enjoy baked treats. I was thinking one of us should take up the hobby.*

Sophia returned the laugh. *You think I need a hobby? You have heard I'm a dragonrider in training with a mysterious mission resting on my shoulders, according to Mother Nature.*

I'd heard rumors of that, Lunis agreed coyly.

Just because you've taken up this hobby to create dragon proverbs with an author slash T-shirt business doesn't mean I need side projects, Sophia replied.

I'm just trying to help you live your best life, he bragged.

Then I need you to work on your proverbs because that one about sarcasm didn't have a ring to it at all, Sophia complained. *Maybe say something about how sarcasm is the result of talking to stupid people.*

I don't think you get the point of these dragon proverbs, Lunis argued. *They are supposed to lift people up, not insult them.*

Are you sure that by pointing out their stupidness it won't help? Sophia challenged.

I don't think "stupidness" is a word, Lunis stated.

And yet, you've just used it, Sophia fired back.

I think you misunderstood the context in which I used it.

Sophia held up the homemade eucalyptus bomb she'd made and admired her handy work. *I have no idea if this will work, but it sure is pretty. I should make stuff with my hands.*

Like jewelry, Lunis remarked.

Sophia rolled her eyes. *I was thinking like weapons or explosives or spyware or something cool.*

Bracelets are cool, Lunis disagreed.

You are so strange, Sophia said, going to work building a fire.

I'm going to go be strange while I eat a kangaroo, Lunis offered. *You good down there?*

Yeah, I'm about to be eating corned beef hash, she said, creating a spark and watching the kindling catch.

I think the heat is already starting to get to you, Lunis said dryly. *If you think corned beef is hiding out under that tree, you might be a bit disappointed.*

I can pretend wombat tastes like corned beef, she reasoned.

Aw, you're going to eat a cute little wombat. Lunis sounded offended.

Says the dragon, she fired back. *Who incidentally eats sheep.*

Just the cult ones that want a way out so they can return to the mother ship, Lunis sniffed.

Sophia shook her head and fanned the flames, proud of the fire she'd built. *I don't know what's under the tree, but I'm eating it.*

We shall see, Lunis said, sounding skeptical. *I'll bring you a roo if all else fails.*

Keep your kangaroo, Sophia told him. *I'm having wombat tacos.*

She turned and faced the burrow, her homemade bomb in her hands.

Now let's hope this works, she thought, her stomach starting to growl from hunger.

CHAPTER EIGHT

"Magic," Sophia remarked. She held the handmade bomb close to the flames to get the outer portion to spark. "I don't need no stinking magic. I've got this."

When the casing caught on fire, Sophia threw the eucalyptus bomb into the burrow. She heard it hit the dirt and roll a few feet.

Now was the moment of truth. If this didn't work, Sophia had to figure out another way to catch food. She had to figure out something since she couldn't just bomb holes in the Outback to get lunch.

The bomb exploded just as she had planned—like a fire-cracker, and made the ground and tree rumble.

Sophia withdrew Inexorabilis from her sheath and stood at the ready, waiting for the wombat or whatever to scurry out from its burrow. Maybe it would be a family of rodents and she could make lunches for the week.

A scratching noise followed a small plume of smoke that shot out of the hole. Sophia narrowed her eyes and listened as the noise grew louder and closer.

Something black and furry popped out of the burrow. It was

hard to make out with the smoke surrounding it, but it didn't move like a furry creature.

The mysterious animal made a series of scratching noises as it scurried from the hole. It stayed in the path of the smoke, keeping it partially obscured.

As far as Sophia could tell, it was about the size of a bowling ball, but its limbs were strange and moved at odd angles.

Sophia stepped forward and tried to get a closer look just as a breeze knocked the smoke away and revealed the bizarre creature.

"Oh, hell," Sophia said, backing up a step.

CHAPTER NINE

The creature before Sophia represented a common phobia for most people. Not for Sophia, though. Living with her eccentric sister Reese had broken her of being fearful of spiders. The kooky magician had forbidden anyone in the family to kill any spiders who entered their residence, saying they were good luck.

Reese probably just wanted them for potions, but many did believe having spiders around was good luck. Reese had often said the spiders thought they were roommates and killing or kicking them out was just plain rude.

However, even Reese would have tensed at the sight of the large spider before Sophia. Its beady red eyes were intently focused on the source of what had stirred it from its home.

It regarded her with menace as it ground its pincers angrily, the threat obvious in its actions.

Sophia tightened her grip on her sword and wondered how spider soup would taste.

Soup? Really? Lunis questioned. *In this heat?*

It was more of a joke than a plan, Sophia retorted.

Can you handle that large arachnid, or do you need my help? Lunis asked.

Sophia scoffed. *Go get your roo. I've got the itsy-bitsy spider.*

All right, then, Lunis replied.

Sensing the spider was about to charge and pounce, Sophia prepared her defense.

A cacophony of scratching echoed from under the tree, making the base vibrate more than when she'd bombed it.

The spider froze. Sophia did as well. She held her breath and waited.

When a mound of black spilled out of the burrow, she bit her tongue and cursed under her breath.

CHAPTER TEN

One giant spider wasn't a big deal to Sophia, although it was inevitable she'd break a sweat fighting the thing since she was sweating profusely just standing there.

The hundreds of spiders that had hurried out of the burrow would be much more of a challenge to fight. Based on their angry red eyes and threatening pincers moving back and forth, a battle was imminent.

What about now? Lunis called, having seen the force facing off against Sophia. She backed up, making room for the spiders, which moved in unison like an army getting ready to charge.

I'm good, she lied, watching the sidelines as the spiders forced her back, nearly making her trip.

Her hands were shaking on her sword's hilt, but she kept her breathing steady as she watched for the first attack.

Okay, well, my dinner is hopping away, Lunis began. *Let me know if you have trouble wrestling yours.*

Sophia wasn't worried about wrestling her next meal. For the first time ever, as she looked at a hundred hairy, angry spiders, she was worried about her dinner eating her.

The first spider, maybe the original one that had scurried from the burrow, sprang at her, hopping like a kangaroo and making considerable progress. She brought her sword around like a baseball bat and swung it as the spider screamed like it was sending a volley of insults at its attacker.

The sword connected with the large spider and knocked it several dozen yards.

Home run! Lunis exclaimed.

Sophia rejoiced, feeling the victory run through her. Celebrations were short-lived as three spiders simultaneously jumped at her from three different directions. The scream that shot out of Sophia's mouth was purely reflexive. The attacks that followed absolutely weren't.

Sophia brought Inexorabilis around, bringing it low to hit the first spider on the right, then up to get the one in the middle and low again to get the creature on the far side. This time, the side of the blade didn't hit the monsters, but rather the edge. It sliced through them and the pieces fell to the red earth.

This only seemed to enrage the creepy beasts, which obviously didn't like watching their mates slaughtered. Not taking the hint that Sophia was a force not to be messed with, they all inched forward, making her take another step back.

You sure you don't want some fire? Lunis asked.

You get to fly, Sophia replied. *Who said anything about fire, though? That seems a lot like magic.*

Hey, can I help it if I cough and fire comes out? Lunis argued.

Sophia shrugged and guessed the dragon had found another loophole for using magic, but she wasn't going to chance it and have to start over. *Keep your fire to yourself,* Sophia stated as an idea occurred to her.

The spiders were inching in closer to her, and she sensed they were about to attack, probably all at once. Before that happened, she had to reduce their numbers drastically.

Sidestepping, Sophia was careful to keep the pack of spiders in her sights. They moved in concert with her, scampering to make up for the distance she tried to put between them. They were planning something. Sophia wasn't sure how she knew, but the way they moved in formation told her they were working together—a strange, silent communication obviously happening among them.

Sophia's eyes darted to the fire she'd made when it was to the side of them.

The arachnids' gazes shifted to the fire as if they were figuring it out.

These were smart, magical spiders, she guessed.

I don't see why I don't get to use magic when I'm fighting a bunch of magical creatures, Sophia complained. She was going to have to make her move soon.

Because life isn't fair, Lunis said. *On a side note, kangaroo tastes pretty good. Could use some barbeque sauce, though.*

What does it taste like? Sophia asked, careful not to give the spiders any hint of what she was planning.

Kind of like venison and buffalo, Lunis described.

You've had buffalo? she questioned.

No, but an ancestor did, he replied.

Sophia nodded, and to her surprise, all the spiders nodded too, copying her movement. "That's odd," she muttered.

They are mirroring you in an effort to understand what you're going to do next, Lunis offered.

Oh, so if I do this... Sophia said, sidestepping three feet to the right.

All the spiders followed her action, hurrying in the same direction.

She jumped and the spiders all hopped.

I don't get it, Sophia mused to her dragon.

I don't think they do either, Lunis said. *Try doing something defensive.*

Okay, Sophia said, taking a step backward.

All the spiders took one step in her direction.

Okay, Lunis said, intrigued. *Now try doing something offensive.*

Sophia lifted Inexorabilis.

The spiders all posed, rising up on the tips of their legs and growing taller.

What does this mean? she asked Lunis.

It means that with what you're planning, Lunis answered, *you better be ready for retaliation. They will respond to you in kind. Retreat, and they will follow. Try to get away, and they will match your movements. Attack, and they will, too.*

What if I smile at them and give compliments? Sophia questioned.

You can try it, Lunis answered.

"Hey, guys," Sophia began with a smile. "You all sure are interesting."

All the spiders crouched like they were part of the same beast. Their red eyes bulged as they hugged the ground, and they appeared like they were about to spring.

No compliments, Lunis exclaimed. *They don't like to be softened up.*

"You guys sure are ugly," Sophia spat, grimacing at the angry spiders.

To Sophia's surprise, a dozen of the giant spiders hopped into the air and fell back down, landing on their backs with their legs flicking like they had just kicked the bucket.

Can this be possible? she asked the dragon.

Interesting, he mused. *It appears that like the old adage, words do break their bones.*

That's so odd, Sophia mused, edging farther to the side. The remaining spiders copied her movement. *So if I run, they'll follow. If I attack, they'll retaliate. And if I criticize them, they'll kick the bucket.*

Yes, but I'd warn you against throwing out a bunch of insults, Lunis said. *There are a lot more of them than you, and I don't think you can kill them all with words.*

What makes you think that? she asked.

Well, try it, he suggested.

Sophia focused on the family of angry spiders. "Hey, guys, you sure are pretty dumb."

Again, a dozen spiders jumped and then landed on their backs, their legs kicking. However, three of the largest flew straight at her face. She screamed, ducking as the first passed over her head. One went by her arm, scratching her with its long pincers. The other attached itself to her leg, holding on furiously with its legs.

"What?" she exclaimed. "Get off!"

Sophia threw a punch at the spider's head as it sank its teeth into her leg. She screamed from the pain, her voice echoing over the Outback.

Hey, you scared the kangaroo away, Lunis complained.

Sophia raised her sword and thrust it down like a toothpick, spearing the spider attached to her and making it release her. Instantly, her leg throbbed from the bite.

Sorry, not sorry, she said to Lunis. *What's the deal with these things.*

Some appear to be copycats, Lunis stated. *Some are young enough that they are hurt by words.*

And the rest? Sophia said, backing up and watching as the two other spiders who had attacked her rejoined the group.

They are murderous and out for blood, Lunis told her. *It's pretty interesting because just one approach won't work on these guys. If you attack, some will retaliate. If you insult, some will die.*

And if I retreat? Sophia suggested, favoring her leg as she sidestepped.

Then they are going to come after you and most likely attack, stripping the flesh off your bones, Lunis explained.

Sophia gulped. *Okay, then it's time for a two-pronged approach.*

I like it, Lunis said, already privy to her idea by spying her thoughts. *Fight the aggressive ones with force and the sensitive ones with words, but you better be fast because one false move and you're spider food.*

Thanks, Sophia said, grateful to be in position. All of the spiders' eyes were locked on her, even though the small campfire she built stood between her and them. They didn't seem to notice, or maybe they didn't realize she had positioned herself there for a specific reason.

She was absolutely certain they knew what she was planning when her eyes skipped to the homemade eucalyptus bombs lying a few feet away. She'd made extra, not knowing if the first would be enough. Now she was glad she had.

They all tensed, about to spring in her direction in a collective attack.

Sophia moved fast, using the speed of the chi of the dragon to drop her sword and grab a bomb in each hand. She hurled them at the spiders, ensuring they passed through the fire on their way.

"You hairy little beasts need a total makeover," Sophia spat as the bombs exploded in the pack, sending up spider parts. The guts rained down from the sky, landing all around the survivors. Several sprang up like popcorn kernels and landed on their backs.

That's *your insult?* Lunis asked with a laugh. "You need a makeover?" *Why don't you tell them they are only of average intelligence?*

Sophia had four more bombs. She launched two of them as the creatures broke out in total chaos.

I'm a bit preoccupied here, Sophia retorted as another dozen spiders exploded. *Why don't you be in charge of the insults?*

I can do that. Lunis chuckled. *Say something about their mom. They probably all have the same one.*

I don't think spiders care what you say about their mom, Sophia argued.

It's worth a shot, Lunis offered as she darted for the last of the bombs. The closest spider tried to cut her off, leaping in her direction and shooting a strand of silk at her. She ducked and kicked the creature like a football, knocking it into the trunk of the tree that was its home.

It squeaked as it landed on the ground next to the two dozen spiders who remained, their red eyes all on Sophia. She bounced the last remaining bombs in her hand, knowing she needed to make the last attack spot on or risk being eaten alive.

"Hey, where's your momma?" Sophia asked, which made all the spiders tense. They tilted their heads in unison, their eyes enlarging like they wanted to hear what she was going to say next. "Yo momma is so fat, she can't even jump to conclusions."

Oh, no. Lunis growled in disappointment.

What? Sophia questioned as the spiders scampered forward, none of them dying.

Try again, the dragon encouraged.

"Fine," Sophia began, pulling her arm back and launching one of the bombs. It landed in the middle of the horde, exploding a dozen spiders and sending guts all over her boots. She sneered. "Yo momma's so stupid, she stared at a cup of orange juice for twelve hours because it said, 'concentrate.'"

Wow, that was bad, Lunis said.

I'm sort of busy right now, she argued, firing her last bomb through the fire and exploding another dozen spiders. There were only about ten left, but Sophia was out of bombs, and her insults didn't seem to be working.

She backed over to her sword and they all copied her movement.

"Yo momma…" Sophia began, kneeling, her arm outstretched.

Before she could think of her next insult, something bigger than all the rest of the spiders surfaced from the burrow. It seemed to have trouble pushing itself through the hole, its legs long, and its body the size of a beach ball. The thing was hairier than the others, its face elongated, and its red eyes large and menacing.

"Whoa!" Sophia said, nearly tripping over her feet as she backed up. She looked the large spider over. "Yo momma is so ugly, she makes you all look adorable."

CHAPTER ELEVEN

The ground shook under Sophia when the ginormous spider took a step forward, its pincers working.

That is one ugly spider, Lunis declared.

Tell me about it, Sophia said, landing in bug guts with her next step. This seemed to add insult to injury, and the momma spider scuttled forward, moving fast across the dirt.

Sophia barely had enough time to bring up Inexorabilis before the spider was on her. Its pincers were inches from her throat when she threw up her blade.

She held her sword like a shield, trying to push the beast back by kicking its large body. Its legs reached for her on either side of the blade, but it didn't try to come any closer.

There's something about the sword that repels it, Lunis stated.

Sophia waved the blade like a torch, and sure enough, the spider retreated a few inches.

"Hey, Momma, you're so ugly that if you threw a boomerang, it would refuse to come back," Sophia said, swinging Inexorabilis and making the monster jump back to avoid getting cut.

I don't think insults work on Momma, Lunis suggested. *Or maybe your jokes are just not good enough to be offensive.*

Sophia spied the spider sending a shot of silk in her direction just in time to dive out of the way. It hit the fire, putting it out completely. She rolled over and sprang to her feet.

So she doesn't like Inexorabilis, Sophia mused, trying to figure out her options. She didn't have any more bombs or fire.

You can call your trusty dragon, Lunis hinted.

He's busy eating a steak dinner, she replied. *And he's way over there on the other side of the Outback.*

He could come back in a few seconds, he promised.

And what, take all the fun? Sophia said, feigning to one side and trying to throw Momma off. The spider didn't fall for the trick and instead thrust one of her many long legs into Sophia's side with surprising force and making her hit the side of the tree with a thud. That was the source of her current dilemma.

That's going to leave a mark, Lunis said.

Sophia shook her head and tried to push up but found Momma bearing down on her, literally breathing down her neck.

"Hey," Sophia said nervously, smelling the rancid breath of the beast that was about to slit her neck. The impact with the tree had been more than disorienting, and Sophia realized she'd dropped her sword.

Her fingers scrabbled through the dirt, finding only bug guts. She whimpered as the spider bore closer to her, its pincers making promises she couldn't understand but got the gist of.

Soph, Lunis said, a question in his voice, *you still got this?*

She shook her head erratically.

"No!" she exclaimed, abandoning all attempts to be a lone badass. "Help, Lunis!"

She expected it would take him a bit to rescue her. Momma would sink her teeth into her and that would be the end of it, but before she even had a chance to suck in a breath, the giant spider was hurled off her.

Sophia caught a glimpse of her blue dragon, the body of the spider in his mouth, before he jerked his head up and to the side, releasing Momma. She landed fifty feet away on the red earth in a cloud of dust and exploded, green goo spraying around her, sending a rancid smell through the hot air.

CHAPTER TWELVE

R agged breath spilled over Sophia's cracked lips, making her chest rise and fall rapidly as she tried to process what had just happened.

Lunis glanced over his shoulder as the mound of spider melted into the earth, steam rising up from the carcass. Casually he turned back to Sophia, a sly grin on his face.

"How long had you been there, waiting for me to ask for help?" she asked.

"Since pretty much the beginning, lurking in the shadows," he replied.

Pushing up, she tried to dust herself off, to no effect. "There aren't any shadows to lurk in around here."

He nodded. "Yeah, it's probably the middle of the day," he observed. The sun was high in the blue sky, not a cloud in sight.

"You didn't think I could do it?" Sophia asked, covering her nose against the putrid smell that filled the air. The dead spider bodies were starting to cook, between the hot ground under them and the scorching rays of the Australian Outback sun above. "You didn't think I could take out the colony of spiders?" She couldn't keep the offense out of her voice.

"Of course, I did," he argued, looking around. "And you obviously did just fine on your own, judging by this aftermath. Do you think we can eat spider? Because if so, we've got food for days. Maybe we jelly them. How do you think spider jam tastes on toast?"

Sophia grimaced. "Ew, that sounds horrible. I refuse to eat spiders, and besides, we don't have any toast."

Sensing she was still upset, Lunis centered his attention on her. *I knew you'd be okay on your own—*

"Okay?" she questioned. "Like I'd get by until I needed you to rescue me?"

Sophia couldn't help it. She knew she was being unreasonable, but it felt right to her. Maybe it was the heat or the hunger or the thirst or the fact her leg was throbbing. She suddenly remembered being bitten and jerked her attention down. Her pants were torn where the teeth of the spider had sunk into her flesh. Green goo swam around the bloody wound in her leg. It didn't look good. Maybe it was the sight of her injury or the poison from the spider, but something made her head swim suddenly with dizziness.

Sophia, I knew you could handle the spiders, Lunis said, his voice comforting, his attention on her wound. *But we are supposed to be able to rely on each other. That's what I'm there for—to help.*

Sophia took a step and instantly regretted it. The lack of adrenaline made the pain in her leg fully apparent. "You never need me to save you, Lunis!"

I haven't yet, he reasoned. *But we have many years for that to change. We're a partnership. I can't do things you can and vice versa. So what that I stepped in at the last moment and saved you? You cleared a hundred spiders on your own using your ingenious bomb-making skills and quick thinking.*

Sophia gave him an annoyed expression. "I insulted them with yo momma jokes."

But you figured out one of their weaknesses, Lunis said.

"Yeah, I guess," Sophia said with a sigh, not at all feeling better.

What do you want me to say? Lunis asked, his expression hard. She knew he was exhausted too, but for different reasons. His belly was full, and his body was used to extreme heat. Because she was connected to the dragon, she knew he was taxed from worry about her, having to watch her battle the spiders and stay back until she asked for help. This just made her angrier.

"I want you to tell me the truth," she argued. "You didn't think I could handle the momma spider by myself."

Lunis shook his head. *You know what's in my head. Do you really hear me saying that?*

Sophia studied him, realizing that his mind was completely open for her to explore. She had tiptoed through his mind many a time, but usually only went as far as to read the thoughts he supplied her. When they scried, she saw what he saw. But in this rare instance, she had full access to his mind. And there it was, sitting neatly on top.

Sophia bit her lip and tasted blood. Her skin was already painfully cracked from the heat. "You thought I would need your help to defeat her."

I thought you could handle her, Lunis argued. *But to defeat her, yes. I thought after battling her children, you'd need some help. It doesn't mean you couldn't do it, but you might have gotten seriously injured.*

She threw her hand at her injured leg. "What do you call this? I'm trapped in the Outback with a poisonous bite and a dragon who doesn't think I can fight on my own! And it smells horrible!"

That's because someone got bug guts everywhere, Lunis said with a laugh in his mental voice.

His attempt at humor wasn't going to work on Sophia right then. She swung around and charged off for the lake, needing some space.

Soph! Lunis called after her.

She didn't turn around. Right then, she needed to be alone. She needed to figure out why she was so angry. And she needed to fix her leg…without magic.

CHAPTER THIRTEEN

I t didn't matter that Sophia knew she was being unreasonable. Her ego was instigating this fight, the first one she'd ever had with her dragon. And yet, there was nothing she could tell herself to just get over it.

She dragged herself to the lake without turning around even though she could feel Lunis staring at her retreating back.

They needed each other in the Australian Outback. They needed to bond to pass the training—more so than ever before. They needed one another to survive the week.

The issue was that she firmly believed Lunis would survive fine without her. Sophia felt like the weak link. She was the one who needed her dragon in order to survive, and it made her feel entirely worthless.

She settled down on a rock next to a clear shore of fresh water and hesitated before submerging her leg. Sophia was aware there could be all sorts of flesh-eating bacteria in the water. Or as was more in line with her luck, piranhas were probably swimming around, waiting to chew off her leg once she stuck it into the lake.

It was throbbing with so much pain she really couldn't handle it any longer. Ripping her pant leg all the way up to the knee, Sophia nearly passed out at the sight of the bite. It was oozing with green slime and quickly swelling.

She refused to look back over to the tree where she knew Lunis was stationed, regarding her like a lost puppy. Sophia didn't want her puppy. She wanted not to need her puppy. She wanted her puppy to need her a tiny bit.

Sophia was the vulnerable human, who might have extra magical powers thanks to those she'd inherited from her twin, but they did her no good out in the Australian Outback when she wasn't allowed to use magic. She sighed with defeat.

She was just a girl here. Nothing special. No unique talents. Just a plain, old girl.

"Without magic, I'm just a loser," she said, sinking her leg into the water and finding it strangely cool even though the heat outside was so high. The water wrapped around her wound and instantly provided relief.

"Without water, I'm a total loser," a voice said in front of Sophia.

Her eyes snapped open. She hadn't even realized they were closed or that she was close to dozing off, the sun making her lightheaded.

She searched around, thinking maybe it was Lunis talking, although the voice was higher pitched than his.

He was still by the tree and currently kicking around in the dirt and launching bits of spider carcasses across the Outback—apparently letting off steam, which ironically was spiraling through the air, coming from the body parts littering the ground.

Yanking her focus back in the direction of the voice, Sophia looked around until she found a pair of eyes resting above the water, a long tail swooshing back and forth a little behind it.

She pulled up her legs, worried she was about to be eaten by the crocodile swimming in the water before her. To her shock, it smiled at her, its eyes not at all appearing hungry like she would have thought.

I'm not going to eat you, the crocodile sent to her mind as if it had read her thoughts. *I don't want to die.*

Sophia's leg hurt outside the water, and since she was hallucinating, she sank it back down into the cool lake. "Who are you?" she asked. Talking to a crocodile was not the strangest thing to happen to her that day, one in which she made homemade bombs from a eucalyptus tree and fought a hundred large spiders. Oh, and had an argument with a dragon. Her life was so bizarre.

I'm Smeg, the crocodile replied. *I mean, I go by many different names, but that's the one the Beaufonts know me by.*

Sophia knew she was hallucinating badly, but she decided to embrace it. *Why not*, she thought. She was going to die in the Australian Outback from a spider bite, talking to a croc.

"Beaufonts?" she asked, thinking it would be fun and take her mind off her pain to indulge the croc. This hallucination, fueled by her imagination, was probably going to be pretty entertaining. "You've met others in my family?"

Well, most recently, Warrior Liv Beaufont in the swamps of Louisiana, Smeg answered.

Sophia shook her head. How dumb her subconscious was that it hadn't figured out this horrible logistic issue with its hallucination. "If you recently met Liv in Louisiana, how are you here in the Australian Outback? Did you fly?"

He chuckled. *Don't be ridiculous. I'm a crocodile. Of course, I can't fly.*

"Right, what was I thinking," she said, shaking her head. "So, how did you get here?"

Magic, he answered. *I go wherever I think I'll find the most entertaining conversations. You see, that's usually what I'm after. Have you heard any fun facts lately? I really like learning things. Oh, and I like words. My new favorite one is "conundrum." Just say it. It feels funny on your tongue.*

Sophia gave him a questioning expression. "You're a very strange croc."

He nodded, water splashing up around his head. *It's true. I'm the strangest. Not like the other crocodiles. None of them talk to me, but they are boring anyway. Most of them never travel.*

Sophia shook her head, her mouth parched. "You're a magical crocodile who talks and travels, is that right?"

Yes, and you're a dying magician on a walkabout in the Australian Outback, right? he asked.

Sophia laughed morbidly. "You've figured me out."

I love playing these kinds of guessing games, Smeg said, circling around in the water and obviously excited to have made a new friend.

"Yeah, it's a delightful game," Sophia said, looking longingly at the water.

I wouldn't drink the lake water, Smeg offered like he knew what she was thinking. He was a figment of her imagination, so what did it matter.

"Why?" Sophia questioned. "Because it's going to kill me?"

Exactly, he answered.

"As you previously mentioned, that's not so much a problem for me since I've been bitten by a poisonous spider and will probably die from it," Sophia stated dully, swaying slightly.

Oh, that's not why I thought you were going to die. Smeg's eyes darted to Sophia's leg and he grimaced. *Tough luck on the bite. Yeah, you'll probably die from that, but not before you are eaten by the hungry dragon over there. That was why I wasn't going to try to eat you. I didn't want the dragon to get mad at me for taking his meal. Oh, well, and you're more use to me as a conversationalist than as food.*

Sophia followed his gaze and saw Lunis still stalking her from a distance. "Oh, that's my dragon. I don't think he's going to kill me. Maybe, though. I did yell at him."

Oh, I didn't realize it was a domestic dispute, Smeg said. *Yeah, he's probably going to kill you. Domestic stuff gets the most out of control. Believe me, I know.*

Sophia couldn't help but laugh. "How do you know?"

I'm a good listener, Smeg offered. *Anyway, yeah, you'll probably die from the bite first. Within the day. I can tell your sister Warrior Beaufont if you want, if she visits a large body of water soon. Do you know what her travel plans are?*

Sophia gripped her leg, the pain starting to shoot upward. "Sorry, I'm not aware of her upcoming plans. Right now, I'm more concerned about funeral arrangements."

Well, you don't have to die, Smeg offered. *I have a solution.*

That got Sophia's attention. "I don't want to die. What can I do?"

Use magic, Smeg said with satisfaction.

Sophia laid back on the rock and looked up at the blue sky. "Yeah, well, I guess I'll die."

She knew they could start over with the training. Maybe that was what needed to happen. She already felt like such a failure. She really didn't want to die as one too. The Australian Outback was supposed to be hard. If it wasn't, it wouldn't be such an important part of the training.

To cure yourself, you just have to go over there and collect one of those dead spider bodies, mix it with some of the plants over there. He indicated a brightly colored bush in the distance. *And then it's a simple spell. So easy.*

"Cool," Sophia agreed. "I'll get right on that as soon as the world stops spinning."

So you and your dragon are mad at each other, Smeg stated, rather than asking.

"Really, I'm just mad at him."

Oh, what did he do? Smeg asked. *Did he steal your boyfriend? Talk about you behind your back? Put you off for another dragon?*

Sophia shook her head and wondered what the hell was wrong with this strange magical crocodile. "No, he saved my life."

No. He. Didn't, Smeg said, punctuating each of the words.

Sophia sighed. "I know it sounds dumb, but we are supposed to be a partnership, and I ride him because I'm little and can't fly. He has the fire powers, and when everything is dire, he swoops in and saves the day. All I do is act sassy and navigate. I'm pretty worthless in this partnership."

Smeg nodded, seeming to understand her plight. *Yeah, you don't seem to be carrying your own weight.*

"Thanks," she said dryly, biting on the word.

Have you considered letting him ride you? he asked.

Sophia gave the magical creature a long, annoyed stare. "You do get that there is a size difference, right?"

Oh, sure, I guess if those are your limitations, he answered. *I'm just trying to help you troubleshoot this problem.*

"There's no troubleshooting it," Sophia said melodramatically, her head feeling full of hot lava. "I'm the invalid human, and he's the awesome dragon. He can fly. I can sit. He can hunt. I can get bitten. He can withstand the elements and know everything from the dragon's consciousness. I can school him in a game of *Mario Kart.*"

Sophia knew riders and dragons had been working together in a mutual partnership for hundreds of years. She'd never read anything in the *Incomplete History of Dragonriders* about ego problems and riders feeling marginalized. Yet, Sophia was the first female rider, and she had feelings. *Maybe that was the problem, though,* she reasoned. Maybe something would be in *The Complete History of Dragonriders,* although she was still waiting to get the book back from Trinity.

When you put it that way, Smeg began, *I totally get your point.*

Sophia nodded, wishing more than anything she had a glass of water. "Yeah, I'm the worst. He's the best. I'm lame. He's awesome, and—"

Before the poison totally takes you out, you mind if I share something with you? Smeg asked.

"Well, when you put it that way, yeah, whatever."

Dragons are much stronger and more powerful than magicians, Smeg explained. *They are the strongest magical creatures on this planet. In comparison, magicians are extremely vulnerable.*

"Your speech isn't helping as much as you might think," Sophia remarked.

I apologize. I dropped out of college because of a class I had to take for public speaking, the croc admitted. *Anyway, regardless, why do you think dragons chose to be partnered with humans, knowing humans were the much weaker species?*

The poison in her body made it difficult to think, so Sophia simply shrugged. "I don't know."

You have your own advantages, Smeg explained. *He might be able to fly or withstand high temperatures or tear things apart with his claws. But humans, I think if you really meditate on this, you'll find you offer something crucial for you two. Without it, not only would your dragon not live as long, but more importantly, his life wouldn't be as fulfilling. It's important when considering the value of a partnership that we do not get stuck on the strength one provides and overshadow the traits another gives. Reason can often be considered just as important as power. Strategic thinking, I'd contend, is a superior skill to prowess. Knowing how to combine the skills of a magician with a dragon, well, I think that's something only a human can truly do because they know how to compromise, which is not something the dragon readily understands. If they do, it's only because of the influence of said human.*

Smeg swam in a circle, flicking his tail playfully upon the surface of the water. *Anyway, just my two cents for what they are worth. Really, what do I know? I've just been around for a few hundred centuries, having random conversations with tons of beings through time.*

Sophia swayed, the scenery in front of her blurring as her vision dimmed. "Yeah, what do you know, O strange figment of my imagination?"

Sophia, Smeg insisted, *I'm real. Everything I've said is true. If it weren't, then how would I know every dragon and rider has gone through similar internal conflicts?*

She pointed at him, feeling drunk. "Because that's what I want you to tell me, so I don't feel like such a failure."

But you aren't, Smeg argued. *You, just like Hiker Wallace and Bell, are going through the first feud of many.*

Sophia laughed. "Oh, good job, subconscious. You had the imaginary talking croc bring up Hiker and Bell to legitimize the strange message from my made-up hallucinations. Good one."

Okay, I can see you've already figured this all out, Smeg said, churning something under the water and making the lake swirl.

"Yeah, that's right," Sophia said triumphantly. "I can't fool myself."

No, you can't. A large clump of something like seaweed shot out of the water beside Smeg and landed with a splat next to Sophia.

She was so out of it she hardly budged when the pile of wet weeds landed just behind her on the rock. "What's that for?"

For when you pass out, so you don't bust your head open on the rock, Smeg said thoughtfully.

She smiled. "Thanks. But I'm okay. I'm going to hang out with you, my alter ego, and talk for a bit longer."

Sounds good, Smeg said. *I like talking.*

Sophia swayed and thought how nice it was her hallucination had created a pillow for her, although she wouldn't need it. Then her hand slipped out from under her, and her eyes closed as she fell into blackness.

CHAPTER FOURTEEN

The sopping mossy thing under Sophia's head smelled like fish. She was lying flat on the rock, sort of.

"Hold still, would you?" a familiar woman's voice said just in front of Sophia.

The bright sunlight made it incredibly hard for Sophia to open her eyes. The searing pain on her leg made it a lot easier when she sprang up to a sitting position, clutching her calf.

"Now, now," the woman said. "Leave me to it, would you?"

Sophia blinked. She really was hallucinating to find Bermuda Laurens, the giantess author of *Mysterious Creatures*, hovering and casting a shadow down on her.

"Oh, first a talking croc and now this," Sophia said, throwing herself back, the seaweed cushion softening her fall.

Bermuda, who was wearing a brown safari outfit and hat, turned for the lake. "Smeg was here? Of course, he was! That chatty Kathy. I bet he talked your ear off."

Sophia pushed up to a sitting position. "When I die, will the hallucinations stop?"

Bermuda shrugged. "I don't know. It will be a while before you have an answer since today isn't the day you die. Nor anytime soon, I believe." The giantess was still tending to Sophia's leg, although it progressively hurt less with every passing moment.

"What do you mean?" Sophia asked. "I've been bitten by a magical Outback spider. I'm going to die from this unless I can gather that plant over there and mix it with the dead spiders and a bit of magic."

"Right," Bermuda chirped, shaking off her hands after bandaging Sophia's leg. "Which is what I've done."

Sophia's vision cleared all at once, and she realized what she was seeing was actually real. "You're here! You are actually here with me in the Outback!"

Bermuda looked around, shaken by Sophia's sudden outburst. "Do you mean me?"

Sophia nodded profusely. Her vison was clear, although her mouth still felt like chalk.

"Of course, I'm here," Bermuda confirmed. "And a good thing. I found you passed out, minutes away from a coma. Strangely, I don't remember the path which took me to you or how I got here entirely." Her gaze redirected as she looked to where Lunis was still hiding by the tree. "Oh, but of course, dragons can do all sorts of things when they want to save their rider, like call to those who can help them by using the chi of the dragon…"

"What?" Sophia asked, looking around. "Lunis called you here? But you can't be here. I'm on a walkabout. He is too. Did you use magic on me? Oh no, it's all over!"

Bermuda watched as Sophia threw her fist down on the rock and then grimaced from the act.

The giantess said, "When you're done, I have something to say."

Sophia squirmed for several moments before making her face straighten. "What is that? And are you certain you're not a figment of my imagination?"

"Quite," Bermuda answered. "And you didn't use magic.

Neither did Lunis, although he is magic, so it's hard for him not to use it. Just feeling things, like what he did that drew me to you, is magic. That's the way of dragons. But you shouldn't have to worry about it ruining your training. You didn't perform magic to heal yourself. I found you passed out and fixed you without your consent. You can't be blamed for that."

Sophia nodded and wiggled her toes, noticing the feeling coming back in her leg. "What are you doing in the Outback?"

"I can't tell you that," Bermuda said flatly, holding out a cup to Sophia. "You can have this because I've given it to you, and if you don't drink it, I'll knock you out, and you won't survive the Outback."

Sophia didn't need many reasons for water when she was parched, but she was grateful Bermuda was making her feel less like a loser for having help on her walkabout.

"You really found me, and your help is okay?" Sophia asked, draining the cup.

Bermuda took it back when it was empty. "Yes, and in the future, you'll want to boil the water in this lake for your supply, especially if Smeg was in it."

"Thanks," Sophia said, feeling more herself, although her stomach growled almost on cue to remind her its needs hadn't been met yet. "I don't suppose you can feed me without breaking the rules too?"

Bermuda shook her head, surveying the area. "No, I'm sorry, I can't do any more in good conscience. You were moments away from passing out just now from dehydration, hence the water. The injury, well consider that coincidence. I've done this all for you so far, and therefore you can't be blamed. But if this is a real walkabout, the challenges you face and overcoming them are part of your journey. I can't short you of that."

"Well, I did slaughter a hundred spiders," Sophia confessed.

"Yes, the rarest Spindle spider," Bermuda said bitterly. "I'd be angrier about this except after decades of searching for the creature I have some samples I can study. At least I've made progress, although I'm certain you've just moved them from endangered to extinct."

"Oops," Sophia said. "Blame Lunis. He killed the momma."

"That's why he's over there sulking," Bermuda observed. "Dragons are so very sensitive."

"They are?" Sophia asked and then shook her head. "No, he's over there sulking because I'm a jerk who got mad at him for saving my life."

For all Bermuda Lauren's calloused behavior, she nodded quite sympathetically. "It's hard being the more vulnerable one in a relationship which is supposed to be a partnership. But the shortcoming is yours, my dear. Once you realize your unique gift, your importance, then all those problems will disappear. For now, you're wrestling with your demons, not his."

Sophia mulled that over, recognizing how much sense it made the more she thought about it. The advice was very similar to what Smeg had told her.

She was grateful Bermuda was there and had found her. She wanted to talk to the wise giantess more and have her explain this new realization to Lunis and share other insights. "Will you stay for dinner? I don't know what we're having, but I'm obviously cooking."

Bermuda backed away and shook her head. "Oh, no. I have an expedition awaiting me, and you have a walkabout to continue. You're entitled to a guest here and there on your travels, but at the end of the day, it needs to be just you and Lunis. But I'll see you again soon, Sophia Beaufont. There is little that can keep our paths from intertwining."

"So, it's okay that we spoke?" Sophia asked, still worried she'd done something wrong to end her training.

"It's impossible for a person such as yourself to go anywhere, even a place as remote as the Outback, and not meet someone," Bermuda explained.

"But I was told I couldn't speak to anyone," Sophia argued.

"Yes, meaning you couldn't seek out anyone, but so far, it seems as though I've been the one talking to you." She shrugged. "Besides, a walkabout is not about being away from others. It's about learning how to be with yourself, which it sounds like you're getting a new course on."

"Yes, my demons have come out on this trip."

"Embrace them," Bermuda offered. "Invite them in and talk with them. It's only then you can send them on their way."

"That's lovely advice," Sophia said.

"And it's all you get until the next time, my dear." Bermuda looked out at the seemingly endless terrain and sighed. "Do try to not die or get maimed. The world needs you, Sophia Beaufont."

She offered a tentative smile. "I'll try."

"Well, goodbye for now." The giantess gave her a rare smile and strode away, the Australian Outback swallowing up her large form as she disappeared into the unforgiving landscape.

CHAPTER FIFTEEN

Sophia was hesitant to slide off the rock and onto her injured leg but knew she couldn't hang out by the lake forever, like a lost mermaid.

Lunis was waiting for her. She needed water. And there was a lot more they needed to do if they were going to survive the Australian Outback together. But first, Sophia had to eat crow and say some things to her dragon.

She felt like the proverbial mermaid taking her first step onto the ground. To her surprise, her leg wasn't throbbing. A bandage covered the wound, which would hopefully keep it clean from infection. It also kept it away from Sophia's eyes, which was probably a good thing.

Her first step was a bit wobbly, but when she resigned to trusting her leg and whatever Bermuda had done to heal her, the next several steps were much smoother.

With a tentative glance back at the lake, Sophia said in a hush, "Thank you."

If it hadn't been for Smeg and Bermuda...well, she'd be heartbroken and close to dead. She really didn't think Lunis would let her die there on the rock, but with the anger boiling inside of her, there was little he could do to get her cooperation.

Sophia understood then how resentment and bitter feelings spoil relationships. They wall off the heart so little good can come through. Without heart, a person simply grows cold inside, losing track of what matters most—love.

Being cold right then in the actual sense would have been good. Instead, it was the peak of the day, and with the sun barreling down on her, she thought her boots might melt right off.

The tender expression full of hurt and longing Lunis flashed Sophia as she approached nearly made her crumble like her leg was giving out. She knew what he was feeling because she was feeling it too, not just because of their connection but because she'd caused it.

"I'm sorry," she began when closer. "I—"

We only say sorry when we've done something wrong, Lunis interrupted.

The smell of the rotting spider carcasses was disgusting. Sophia waved away flies and the smell. "I did do something wrong," Sophia admitted. "I lost sight of what's important."

I don't know how frozen yogurt came into this, he teased, instantly lightening the mood.

Sophia flashed him an amused expression. "Lun, what is with you and fro-yo, lately?"

It's the heat making me think of cooler things, he answered.

"I thought you liked things hot, like lava."

He thought for a moment. *I like both. I can withstand the heat, but that doesn't mean I prefer it. I was built to withstand many extremes, but when all is said and done, I prefer our comfortable life together, not because of the posh couches and amenities, simply because of you.*

"Thank you," Sophia began again, hoping Lunis let her get out her rehearsed speech before she forgot it. "I realize my ego—"

It's a good speech, he cut in again, a sneaky expression in his eyes. *But I've already heard it.*

She sighed, knowing keeping things from him was nearly impossible. Lunis knew her thoughts almost at the same time she thought them. Only in conversation when they were bantering back and forth did she give him any surprises.

"Fine, well, I'd know what you were thinking in response to my excellent speech, but I was passed out, and my head is still swimming from the poison," Sophia admitted.

I wasn't going to let you die, he insisted.

"No, you magically called Bermuda Laurens over to save me."

He swished his tail back and forth, creating a welcomed breeze. *She wasn't too far away, and I knew she'd want to see the Spindle spiders.*

"Yeah, she's not as mad as I figured about taking them out." Sophia gazed around at the disgusting mess of dead spiders and wondered why they were hanging out there when they could be just about anywhere else in the Australian Outback.

The other dragons are still of the old mind, Lunis began, his voice careful and very intentional with every word. *They prefer the Cave cold and hard because they believe dragons can't have luxuries, or it makes us soft. They prefer the harsh cold or extreme heat. They crave battle. They think our suffering makes us better, but I think they're wrong.*

Sophia, I've never believed, even with the knowledge I have of my ancestors, that I need to suffer to be a better dragon. Maybe I'm naïve or young or inexperienced, but I've known since the beginning the only thing that makes me better is you.

Sophia tensed inside and held in tears, knowing she couldn't cry—mostly because she needed all her fluids, but also because she didn't want to interrupt.

No, you can't always save me due to our obvious size and magical differences, Lunis continued. *What you do for me is better than swooping into a battle and rescuing me. Every day since I hatched, you've reminded me what is most important in this world. The dragons have almost forgotten, so consumed with experiencing constant suffering. They have their riders but think the humans are to provide perspective and partnership. In all honesty, without you all, we'd lose sight of why we fight, why we started fighting. Dragons have a long history of killing each other and other creatures because of our constant desire for war. We are given our history through the collective consciousness, but it's so long we forget how it started. It is humans—our riders—who remind us why we started fighting. It was for love.*

Sophia's feet brought her forward as Lunis' head lowered. She caught it in her hands and looked deep into his eyes, seeing more than just his pure intention and deep affection for her. Sophia, at that moment, saw the very soul of her dragon—intertwined with hers for all time.

CHAPTER SIXTEEN

N ever again did Sophia want to be mad at Lunis. It felt exactly the same as being mad at herself. Warring with one's self was impossible to win.

She knew there would be other conflicts between her and her dragon. They had to remember they were connected but weren't the same. It was their unique abilities that made them so good for one another.

"Okay, so I vote we move away from the graveyard of gross spider carcasses," Sophia said, still feeling tender and raw inside.

Oh, I thought this was our forever home, Lunis joked. *We'd plant a bed of tulips over there and use the dead bodies of our enemies as fertilizer.*

She laughed. "I don't think tulips or anything that isn't strong and hearty as hell can grow in this place."

We should probably think about food for you before the sun goes down. Lunis' gaze drifted off to the area around the lake where the mountains provided some shelter.

"And we need to set up a camp and start another fire," Sophia offered.

Leave the fire to me, Lunis said proudly.

"No fair," Sophia complained. "You get to fly and use fire and call helpers to you, and it's not considered magic."

And you get to benefit from my loophole, Lunis retorted. *Also, you get to use all your skills and charm because they also aren't considered magic, but we both know better. It's all relative.*

Sophia winked at him. "Good point. Okay, you make a fire over there, and I'll catch something for dinner." She pointed to an area of the rock wall with a series of corners that would be ideal for shelter.

What are you planning for food? Lunis asked, obviously trying to keep his skepticism out of the question.

She pulled her sword from its sheath. "How hard can it be to fish?"

The answer was very hard. It was extremely difficult to fish with a sword. Sophia had remained frozen, standing in the shallow and patiently waiting for a fish to swim by. Then she'd spear her sword at the creature, but it invariably hurried away before being impaled.

You're using force, Lunis said.

Am I supposed to persuade them to jump onto the end of my sword? Sophia joked.

No, but if you soften your mind, you might find attack is more proactive and less reactionary, Lunis offered, gathering wood for the shelter. *The abruptness of your movements frightens the fish. If you strike with more precision and fluidness, they will be speared before they even know what hit them.*

Haha, Sophia replied, laughing at his pun. *Is this like that Bruce Lee, "Become the water" thing?*

Yeah, that works, Lunis replied, starting to arrange his shelter.

Sophia pulled in a long, meditative breath and tried to calm herself. Lunis was right. She had been tensing while waiting for the fish to approach. As soon as she saw one, she threw the sword at it, a very reactionary movement.

Trying not to rush and edging the constant hunger from her mind, Sophia waited for the next fish to swim into her area. It became apparent that when one was hungry, the screaming desire for food made one reckless and drove away that which one wanted. The desperation was a loud siren sending everything nearby into chaos and making it scatter, which wasn't the way dreams were realized.

She breathed when she felt anxious and impatient. She embraced the uncertainty. She invited in the waiting and got comfortable with it. This felt like what she was supposed to do with her demons per Bermuda and Smeg's advice.

Running from one's problems usually only brought them closer. This brought a poem to Sophia's mouth. The words echoed in her mind, although she didn't remember memorizing the words of the great poet Rumi:

"This being human is a guest house.
Every morning a new arrival.
A joy, a depression, a meanness,
some momentary awareness comes
as an unexpected visitor.
Welcome and entertain them all!
Even if they are a crowd of sorrows,
who violently sweep your house
empty of its furniture,
still, treat each guest honorably.
He may be clearing you out
for some new delight.
The dark thought, the shame, the malice.
Meet them at the door laughing and invite them in.
Be grateful for whatever comes.
because each has been sent
as a guide from beyond."

When she'd finished whispering the poem, Sophia found herself close to tears again, amazement dancing in her being. She didn't know how she knew the poem or where it had come from, but its words were perfect and reflected her current evolution.

The chi of the dragon, Lunis offered. *It is connecting you with all.*

Sophia nodded and felt a delightful chill running over her arms even though it was still hotter than hell in the Outback.

"Invite them in," she said mostly to herself, holding her sword and welcoming the impatience. Welcoming her imperfections. Welcoming more failure if that was what it took to get where she needed to go.

She didn't startle like before when a large shiny fish swam into the waters by her feet. Also, unlike before, she didn't plunge her sword into the water, missing the fish and scaring it away.

Sophia didn't move at all. She simply watched the fish peck around at the rocks. She studied it as it curled and moved through the water, managing its path with the current pushing it one way and then another.

To her amazement, Sophia felt no quick impulse to kill the creature she desperately needed for replenishment. Yes, she wanted the fish, but something inside of her had changed. She didn't feel the need to chase it. To trap it before it got away. Deep within her being, she knew the fish was hers, and it would come to her if she simply relaxed.

It was that thought that led to another: All things which were truly hers couldn't be scared away. They were all there for the taking as long as she remained keenly focused on them, knowing they belonged to her.

A man who desperately desires gold pushes it away when he races for it. But the man who knows the gold is already his simply has to shut off the light at night and wait for it to be delivered to his door in the morning.

Sophia had the strange desire to close her eyes as she knelt soundlessly, not disturbing the water where she stood with a single ripple. With her free hand, she reached blindly into the water, not in a rushed movement, but definitely a stealthy one and grabbed the fish, pulling it out of the water and holding it victoriously above her head.

She learned what she wanted was merely a thought away, no more, no less.

CHAPTER SEVENTEEN

The water was boiling over the fire in a large rock Lunis had thrown against the ground and broken to hollow out. The many fish Sophia had caught were roasting over the flickering flames. Rider and dragon were hard at work creating their individual shelters.

Sophia hadn't played with building blocks much growing up, but she was pretty happy with what she'd constructed when she stepped back to admire it. She'd taken a series of sticks and created a rooftop to provide shelter from the unrelenting sun. It was built between the corners of two rock walls to give her protection from multiple directions. It wasn't a resort with central air and plumbing, but it would do until she found more supplies and maybe added another wall and a door.

Lunis stepped even with her, similarly admiring what he'd done. Sophia couldn't help herself. She burst out laughing at the sight of his shelter, nestled adjacent to hers.

What? he asked, sounding offended.

"Let's see how you did," Sophia began, using the voice of the host from Lunis' favorite Netflix show, *Nailed It* where amateur bakers were expected to replicate seriously difficult cakes and follow the complicated design. "This is what you were trying to make." She held her hand out at the shelter she had made, which had a clean design and was practical in every way. "And here's what you made."

The structure Lunis had crafted looked like a bonfire with long logs that poked up in different directions in the corner of his rock wall.

Nailed it, he sang with no enthusiasm.

"Where exactly were you planning on sleeping in there?" Sophia asked, craning her head to check out the awful structure.

"Over there to the left...or right." He shook his head. "I was just going to wedge in there and have the sticks cover me.

"Good idea." Sophia laughed. "But how about you share my structure? It should be large enough for the two of us."

He nodded appreciatively. "It's nice that what I suck at, you do competently."

Sophia admired their camping area as the cooking fish filled the air with a smoky, savory smell. "I agree. Good job to us for surviving the first day."

Only six more to go, Lunis said, settling down close to the flames as Sophia went to work pulling the fish and water off the fire.

She was desperately hungry and thirsty, but it didn't bother her as much because she felt fulfilled from within.

CHAPTER EIGHTEEN

For not having any seasoning, the fish wasn't bad, although Sophia wished she'd eaten fewer bones.

She'd drunk as much water as she could, feeling as though she'd never feel properly hydrated.

You're going to be peeing all night, Lunis said, settling down into the shelter when the sun began to set, sending an array of oranges and pinks across the sky.

The thought of having to venture off into the Australian Outback at night by herself without magic made Sophia set down the bowl of water. She ran her hand across her mouth and realized how dirty she was. Half of her pant leg was missing and there was dirt in every crevice she had, even some she didn't remember having. They had survived the first day, and Sophia was grateful.

She crawled in beside Lunis. He opened one of his wings to create a spot for her just as a chill hit the air, cued by the sun going down.

Sophia could hardly believe how fast it went from hot to cold in the Outback. She nestled into the warmth of her dragon, grateful when he laid his wing over her like a blanket and tucking her into him.

She found her eyes closing as the sounds of the Outback began to hum them to sleep. It was a strangely peaceful arrangement even though they were sleeping in the middle of nowhere after one of the hardest days either had ever experienced.

Sophia listened to Lunis' heartbeat under her ear and found herself smiling about the simple sound that meant the world to her. She cracked her eyes open and spied the stars peeking out in the vast sky. As they said their hellos to the world, Sophia decided it was her time to say goodnight to the Outback.

"Good night, Lun."

Good night, Soph, he said, holding her tightly, sweet need expressed in the small movement.

The growling awoke Sophia, making her stir out of Lunis' embrace. She knew at once he was already awake.

We're surrounded, he told her in her head.

How? Sophia asked, attempting to make no noise as she sat up.

Lunis adjusted to make room for her to move. *I'm guessing because we were both so exhausted that whatever it is got in without waking us. I'm sorry.*

Don't be, she reassured at once, knowing she'd slept through it all too.

Pushing the grogginess from her head, she willed her eyes to adjust to the dark. The fire had burned out, and the Outback was mostly blackness, save for the stars twinkling in the sky.

The growls came from different directions, meaning Lunis was correct. They were surrounded.

What are they? Sophia asked, spying pairs of reflective eyes here and there in the darkness before they jerked away, the animals scampering to the side.

My first guess was dingoes, Lunis responded.

Sophia caught the outline of one of the beasts as they moved closer. It indeed had the hunched back of a dingo, its sharp teeth shining in the darkness. However, when it growled, its eyes glowed red.

Oh, hell, Sophia said, grabbing for Inexorabilis beside her. *Those aren't normal dingoes.*

CHAPTER NINETEEN

The growling was almost deafening as Sophia and Lunis rose to their feet, the rock wall at their backs and an unknown number of enemies spreading out in front of them.

She could hear the strange dingoes charge around them, creating what she thought was an arch from wall to wall. They were, in fact, surrounded.

Sophia wasn't worried. She had Lunis. And Inexorabilis. What she wished, was that she could see something besides the strange flash of red eyes every now and then as the monsters ran past each other, their energy building as they got more excited, feeding off one another's eagerness.

Don't be overly confident, Lunis warned. *Even a regular dingo shouldn't be underestimated when in a pack. They know how to work together to bring down a water buffalo.*

Sophia nodded, knowing he was right. Too much confidence was the curse of any warrior. Sophia's sister, Liv, had told her once, urging her to always remain humble.

We need light, Sophia said.

Well, I could blast them with fire, and then we can go back to sleep, Lunis offered. *I was having this great dream about gorging on nachos and binge-watching the new season of* Lost in Space. *I'd like to get back to that.*

I'd like to get back to that dream too, Sophia related. *However, I don't think blasting fire at these creatures blindly is a good idea. Can you relight the fire?*

You know I can, Lunis said and spat a neat stream of fire in the direction of the campfire, relighting the kindling. It wouldn't last long since it was almost burned out, but it stayed lit long enough for Sophia to make out the details that told her more of the story.

She shook her head and reflexively stepped in closer to Lunis. "Well, of course," she complained, speaking out loud. "They would have to be zombie dingoes."

CHAPTER TWENTY

The fire illuminated a pack of dingoes who were uglier than most, which was saying a lot. Many of their red eyes were hanging loosely in the sockets of their rotting heads. The sides of many of them were missing, their flesh hanging and bones exposed. They were bits of blood and fur, hissing and growling at the pair backed up to the rock wall.

Of course, they are zombies, Lunis echoed. *Why would we expect anything normal at this point?*

Sophia brandished her sword and revolved in a half-circle, doing her best to intimidate each of the dingoes she faced off with. "Right. Well, after magical, giant spiders and talking crocodiles, I really should have expected this. Are there no normal animals out there anymore?"

I don't think the normal ones want anything to do with us, Lunis offered as the howling grew louder.

"Well, any bright ideas on how to deal with these guys?" Sophia asked.

Since they are zombies, I would speculate that killing them won't work, Lunis mused.

Sophia nodded and watched as one of them limped closer,

drool flooding his mouth. "Yeah, they appear to have been killed a few times already."

I guess there's only one way to find out, Lunis remarked. *Shall I?*

Sophia knowing what he was asking, simply nodded.

He opened his mouth and pointed it to the north of their camp area where the pack started and spread out to the other side. After drawing a breath, the dragon sent a roaring blast of fire at the closest zombie dingo. The creature didn't retreat as one would expect.

Sophia watched as it dared to come in closer, jumping straight into their campfire as the flames licked at its body. It growled furiously, crouching low, and preparing to jump in their direction.

Lunis focused on the pack and started to revolve his head to the right to blast the rest of the creatures.

"Stop!" Sophia yelled, her hands vibrating with her sword. "The fire doesn't bother them."

This was abundantly clear when the fire halted, and two dingoes ran around their camp area, flames rising off them as they seemed to get more excited like the party had just started.

The closest one ran straight at them, his red eyes locked on the pair. When he was only a few yards away, he jumped, mouth wide and teeth bared. Flames engulfed him like he was a fireball. Sophia stepped in front of Lunis, trying her best pose of intimidation. She didn't waver as the beast soared straight at her. When it was about to clobber her, she stepped to the side and knocked her blade against the dingo's side. The beast dropped to the dirt, where it rolled, extinguishing some of the flames.

Lunis had come out from the wall and was knocking down dingo after dingo as they tried to attack him from the side. The ones who were on fire had run through the bushes, setting many of them on fire and making the dark night ablaze with orange.

Sophia swung Inexorabilis around, catching a monster in her peripheral as she spun. She stabbed the zombie in the midsection and kicked it off her sword, but that did little to stop it from coming at her again.

It lunged, its teeth nearly grazing her unscathed pant leg. She brought her other foot around and kicked the monster in the head, which seemed only to insult it and make it run back at her faster.

Meanwhile, Lunis was throwing the dingoes two at a time, launching them like softballs. This only seemed to encourage the monsters. As soon as they hit the ground, they were back on their feet and sprinting for Lunis.

Sophia had little time to check on her dragon, as she had two dingoes who were trying to make her into dinner, or a zombie. She knew magic could help her, although she wasn't sure how. There had to be a spell to stop the undead, but she knew magic wasn't an option. She could have turned to magic before, but the point of this exercise was to find other choices.

Giving up now would only make her job harder the next time. It was better to do this right the first time, even if it meant she might get bitten by a zombie. She hoped Bermuda hadn't gotten off too far if that happened, because she would probably need the giantess's help to heal herself, yet again.

CHAPTER TWENTY-ONE

For hours, Sophia and Lunis defended their camp, staying close to each other. Lunis only used fire when it grew too dark to make out their enemies. Lighting them up only seemed to excite the zombies. Still, they both needed the light.

Sophia sliced through the dingoes, but it did little to get rid of them. It seemed to slow a few, but only because it made it harder for them to spring off the ground and attack with their many lacerations or missing body parts. Lunis batted at the dingoes who tried to attack him, but even that became a challenge as his energy waned and theirs didn't.

There were a few desperate moments where Sophia almost resorted to magic when she thought they were about to be ambushed. She watched as a zombie's jaws nearly connected with Lunis' side. If it wasn't for his thick hide, the animal would have bitten him, infecting him with whatever had made it the way it was. In the end, Lunis was able to knock the beast away with a swipe of his tail, sending it into the rock wall, where it slid to the ground before popping back up, ready to keep playing.

Sophia could hardly breathe from the constant fighting and was close to making a costly mistake when the dingo she was fighting backed away, its red eyes narrowed on her like she'd finally done something to offend it.

She glanced at her sword and wondered if Inexorabilis had projected some new power that worked on these strange zombies. That's when she noticed the fires had burned out, but there was an orange light glowing on the horizon.

The sun was rising in the Australian Outback, and with it, the zombie dingoes were retreating, one by one.

The pack hurried away as the bright orange ball that promised to bring sweltering temperatures rose in the distance.

Sophia couldn't believe she was happy to see the sun that would make the day completely intolerable. However, it appeared the zombie creatures didn't do daylight, which meant Lunis and Sophia had some respite until nightfall.

She slumped next to her dragon, lowering her sword for the first time in hours. Her breath was ragged, and the cold chill of the retreating night air grazed over her sweat covered back made her shiver.

Sophia sank against Lunis, who staggered on his feet, exhaustion heavy in his body too. They had survived the night, but now they had another day that would bring its own challenges.

CHAPTER TWENTY-TWO

S ophia yawned, making her dragon copy her.

"How is that gesture even contagious for dragons?" she asked, laughing and wishing she could magic some coffee. She searched the scorched area, her brain looking for some coffee plants she could harvest.

Yawning is universally contagious no matter who you are, but especially if you spent half the night fighting zombie dingoes, he replied.

"If I had a nickel for every time you ever said that..."

You would have a nickel, he retorted.

"Coffee..." Sophia pulled her mouth to the side, thinking. "How do we make coffee from dirt, dry kindling, and a bunch of strange bugs?"

You didn't bring any magic beans with you, did you? Lunis joked.

Sophia shook her head. "If I did, Mahkah would have confiscated them."

She considered convincing Lunis they should duck back into the modest shelter and take a nap, but the temperature was already rising. Sophia knew it would be next to impossible for her to sleep in this heat, especially with Lunis radiating warmth.

There was also the fact they needed to hunt, eat, hydrate, and take care of their other personal needs.

Surviving was exhausting, she thought, pushing her dirty hair out of her face.

Okay, Lunis said, his voice slow and words slurred. *Do you want to be in charge of water, and I'll go and get us a kangaroo to roast?*

Sophia nodded, not even daring to argue she needed to hunt her own food. She'd come so far since the day before when she thought she had to do everything herself, to prove she could survive on her own. The walkabout wasn't about being strong enough on her own. It was about the two of them relying on one another and being strong enough together. Divide and conquer.

Lunis lit a fire before taking off, slumping at first before he recovered. He was fatigued from the long fight, but they would pull through together.

Sophia went to work to collect water to be boiled. It was slow work since she only had so many rock containers. Her pants were drenched within minutes, which reminded her she'd need a bath at some point.

After breakfast, she decided, wondering what her face looked like. She was pretty certain it was covered in dirt, and her hair was matted to her head in different places.

While she was trying to find more rocks to drop on the ground and crack open, to reveal a hollow center that made a nice bowl, Sophia found some pretty gemstones which, if polished, could be really nice. She collected a few and stuck them in her pocket, thinking they might make good jewelry.

She planned on spending the day surviving the Outback, but if the opportunity presented itself, she thought she might take some time to be creative. A nap might not be in her future, but some creative exploits could be her saving grace.

A short time later, Lunis returned, carrying a sizable kangaroo that was thankfully dead. He set it a safe distance away from the camp and went to work cleaning the thing with his claws. Sophia was grateful he was an expert butcher because she didn't want that job. She had collected enough kindling to keep them supplied through the next few days.

The next task was to determine how to protect the camp from the zombie dingoes. It wasn't certain they would be back come nightfall, but it was a safe assumption.

"Can we construct a border fence?" Sophia asked, biting into the meat, its grease dripping down her chin. Without a napkin to sop it up, she was forced to use the back of her hand to wipe it away. Suddenly she felt like one of the guys at the Castle, being all uncivilized.

Lunis thought for a moment as he ate his meat raw, not because he didn't like it roasted or seasoned. He was a cultured dragon, after all. Mostly it was because he didn't want to go to the extra work and said the kangaroo was fine as it was.

We could set some traps for them, he suggested.

"Yeah, that's a good idea," Sophia said. "Like some spikes under the ground and netting, maybe?"

He nodded. *I think it will slow them down, but honestly, it won't stop them. They are unrelenting.*

"Should we consider moving the camp somewhere else?" Sophia pointed up to the top of the mountain. "How about there?"

I think they can climb, Lunis stated. *And I think we're better off being close to our water supply and having the shelter of the mountain at our back. I hate to admit it, but if they could have surrounded us fully we may not have survived.*

Sophia agreed with a nod. She thought the same thing. It had been the only relief they'd had last night when they could put their back to the wall and know they only had to focus on three fronts.

"I wonder what they are all about?" she wondered. "Like, where did they come from, and what do they want?"

Besides to eat us and turn us into zombies? Lunis asked.

Sophia finished her food and washed it down with water. "Yeah, besides that."

I'm not sure, but hopefully they won't be back tonight.

Sophia rose and tried to shake off the dirt, which was sort of a ridiculous notion at this point. "I hope so, too, but if they are, we are going to be prepared."

CHAPTER TWENTY-THREE

L unis and Sophia spent the rest of the day tirelessly setting traps for the zombie dingoes. She used her sword to sharpen stakes he'd then buried under the sand. Later they worked together to create some netting from bushes that had really tangled branches.

Using a rudimentary pulley system, they were able to set the traps up so a single action would activate them and scoop up the trespassing creature.

Sophia was pleasantly surprised by the end of the day that she had gone so long and done so many complex tasks without magic. Their traps were still full of faults, and she and Lunis worried the dingoes were smart enough to get around them.

One of us is going to have to keep watch, Lunis suggested.

"I'll take the first shift," she offered, having never seen him as tired as he was that day.

He didn't argue, probably knowing she wouldn't back down regardless. *Okay, but wake me up in a few hours and I'll take over. And of course, wake me up at the first sign of the dingoes.*

"Hopefully, they will find someone else to torture tonight," she said and settled next to her dragon as the sun set. She patted him affectionately as his heavy eyes closed and sent him straight into dreams.

Sophia knew that last night he could have taken off at any point and escaped the zombies. However, he couldn't take her, and so he'd fought by her side. She hugged into him, feeling more bonded to her dragon than ever before. Sophia hardly thought it possible since she'd known him since birth, and yet, turmoil had brought them closer.

Sophia could have opened a portal and escaped the carnage, but that would have been cheating. They were going to pass this training without breaking any rules. The other dragonriders had, and so would she.

It boggled Sophia's brain that Evan had survived the Outback for seven days when he complained if his toast was room temperature, but she guessed he could weather many different storms when he wanted.

The first watch went without any trespassing by the zombies, at which point Sophia gently woke Lunis and told him it was his turn to take over.

He did so without a word, thoughtfully squeezing her into him with his wing folded around her. Sophia had closed her eyes for less than a minute and was already deep in dreams when Lunis jumped to his feet, blasting fire up to the sky to briefly illuminate their surroundings.

They are back, he said, his words full of anger.

Sophia sluggishly got to her feet, nearly falling on her face. "Of course, they are. I think they are after my beauty sleep."

The dragon flashed her a smile, rejuvenated by his few hours of rest. *You look beautiful. But look alive. Something tells me the beasts are more rambunctious than last night.*

"What tells you that?" she asked over the chorus of growls in the distance, red flashing eyes sparking up the darkness.

Something dropped onto the roof over their heads, nearly making the structure buckle under them.

Sophia was instantly glad they hadn't taken to higher ground with the zombie dingoes jumping into their camp from above. She pulled out her sword, ready for whatever came next.

The dog peeked his head down below the roof as if to say hello, but Sophia wasn't in the mood for unexpected visitors. She brought Inexorabilis up and around, her tiredness making her break through the roof as she sent the mutt tumbling to the ground and rolling toward the perimeter of their camp where he fell onto one of the buried spikes, making him retreat as he howled.

The traps kept the zombies back but didn't deter them entirely. Again, Lunis and Sophia spent the entire night keeping the monsters away. It wasn't until sunrise the strange dogs retreated, leaving the pair more exhausted than the night before. Sophia actually slumped against Lunis, almost asleep on tired feet.

CHAPTER TWENTY-FOUR

You need a nap, he said when all was clear.

She wanted to argue but had no energy to do so. Sophia allowed Lunis to lower her onto the dirt floor of the broken shelter where the sun was already streaming through, threatening any ounce of sleep. She had no idea how she'd rest with the temperature rising and her stomach starting to growl.

Before long, she forgot her troubles and fell into a dreamless sleep.

When Sophia awoke, she was in comfortable darkness. None of it made sense based on what she remembered. Turning over in the dirt, she tried to make sense of her world.

The darkness lifted, and Sophia found she'd been under Lunis' wing, which was nice and cool in contrast to the assaulting heat and brightness of the Australian Outback. It came shooting into her as soon as he pulled his wing away.

Good evening, Sunshine, he said, smiling down at her as she rose.

"Did you say evening?" she asked, stretching and noticing the sun was close to the horizon.

Yes, you missed most of the day, he answered. *But I saved you some roo*. He indicated the fire.

Her stomach lurched with desire at the sight of the roasted meat over the waning fire. "I can't believe I slept the day."

You needed it, he said.

"And you hunted and kept your wing over me?" she asked, going to work on the meat.

Well, not at the same time, he admitted. *I'm sorry. I had to leave you here in the scorching heat while I hunted, but you weren't alone for long.*

"Thank you," she said between bites.

Always, he said at once and then gave their broken structure a regretful glance. *I'm sorry I didn't have a chance to repair our shelter, but even if I had, I'm not sure I could have done much good.*

Sophia laughed. "Yeah, you probably wouldn't have nailed it, but the thought is what counts." She chewed and listened to the strange noises of the Outback for a moment before asking the question on both their minds. "So, tonight…"

Yeah, they will probably return, Lunis replied.

"And you spent all day watching after me and not able to set traps."

No, Lunis argued. *You spent half the night watching out for me. I simply returned the favor, not that there should be any of those between us. I do things for you because I want to, not out of return or obligation.*

"Well, still," Sophia stated. "Night is quickly approaching, and we have no traps, no structure, and I sense the dogs are getting smarter."

Lunis gave her a commiserating expression. *I was thinking the same thing. They seem to learn more each night and come back with better attacks.*

Sophia let out a breath, feeling heavy and lost.

They were exhausted, wrecked from the obstacles of the Outback. And yet, she wasn't even close to quitting. She allowed her mind to trail back to when they started this journey, a long and strangely short three days ago. She'd already learned so much since then and grown so much. She and Lunis had bonded in new ways. She remembered the poem by Rumi, and it washed over her like spring rain, which would have been wonderful, but it was only in the metaphorical sense.

"...an unexpected visitor.

Welcome and entertain them all!

Even if they are a crowd...who violently sweep your house...treat each guest honorably.

He may be clearing you out

for some new delight.

The dark thought, the shame, the malice.

Meet them at the door laughing and invite them in.

Be grateful for whatever comes.

because each has been sent

as a guide from beyond."

Sophia sucked in a breath, not believing what she was about to suggest. Before she could, Lunis rose, casting her in his shadow.

You aren't proposing... he began, sensing her thoughts.

She swallowed. Straightened. Nodded.

"I think we have to allow them into our camp," she stated with confidence. "We can't fight them. We have to welcome our demons."

CHAPTER TWENTY-FIVE

With the broken shelter littering the wall behind them, Sophia and Lunis lay together, both vibrating with anxiety.

It was strange to have options to get out of bad situations and not use them. Lunis could fly. Sophia could portal away. They both had magic. And yet, they were going to lie together and rest while furious beasts they'd battled for hours on end invaded their camp.

The sun's final rays spread across the Outback, making the land glow. Sophia was still exhausted even after sleeping all day. She was certain she'd stay up most of the night since she was too curious to shut her eyes properly.

"You need to sleep, though," she said to Lunis, knowing he was listening to her thoughts.

Just until they arrive, he promised and closed his eyes, obviously tired from the partial night's sleep and the demands of the day.

He was snoring within a minute, a comforting sound that joined the others of the Outback nicely.

When the rabid hounds showed up, Sophia didn't bolt into

position like she had the nights prior. She started to wake Lunis but stopped herself. They weren't fighting the beasts. At least that was the plan, so she didn't see any reason to rouse Lunis from what seemed like pleasant dreams.

She'd heard him mumble polite phrases throughout the night like, "Thank you" and "Yes, please," making her believe he was dreaming of nachos and binge-watching television.

If things got dire, she'd definitely wake her dragon and happily fly off on him, admitting she was wrong. For the time being, he might as well sleep while she decided if her convoluted plan, centered mostly on faith, was correct.

The dingoes did as they had the first night and prowled around the perimeter, their red eyes flashing as they growled and made their presence known.

Sophia watched, her arms around her dragon. For a long while she watched them drawing nearer, taking their chances by inching in closer and closer. Her instinct was to fight. To rise to her feet and swing her sword and tell her dragon to defend.

She resisted and simply lay still, doing her best to ignore the zombie creatures. When they were close enough that she could smell them it was hard not to move, especially when they drew in so close their fur whisked her skin as they passed.

Lunis jumped to his feet and threw Sophia off him when they brushed him.

Sophia tightened her grasp around his neck and held him close. *Don't move*, she encouraged, speaking in his head.

You didn't wake me, he scolded, hurt obvious in his tone.

I'm sorry, she apologized and then shook her head. *No, I'm not sorry. You needed to rest, and there was nothing to see but the creatures stalking us.*

I wanted to see that, he demanded.

You've missed nothing, she stated as one of the monsters sniffed her boot, drool dripping from his mouth.

Lunis eyed the monster, and Sophia knew he was resisting his every instinct by not attacking.

Just allow them, Sophia encouraged.

One of the dingoes ran by, nipping the dragon's tail and darting away. It wasn't enough to draw blood, but it was enough that Lunis' head swung in the direction of the retreating mutt.

Just let it go, Sophia said, observing that since he awoke and started paying attention to them, they had become more rambunctious, just like on the other nights. When they'd fought the beasts, the dingoes got more enlivened. When Sophia was the only one awake, they had been pretty subdued.

Maybe she had been wrong not to wake Lunis, she reasoned, but she'd wanted to give him a chance to sleep. He was on guard now, and that seemed to have an effect on the dogs.

Lun, I think you need to close your eyes and relax.

How can I even consider that, he asked, stress coating his voice.

I know it seems counterproductive, Sophia said. *But that's what my instinct says.*

A pair of rather large zombie dingoes were approaching on either side of them, their fangs bared and their eyes glaring red.

But Sophia, Lunis argued vehemently in her head.

I know, she replied. *But trust me. Close your eyes. Relax. Invite them in.*

She felt Lunis rumble internally with unease. She knew this was against his nature, which always told him to fight. She also knew he trusted her more than anything else. The more she held onto him and encouraged him to relax, the more she knew he was closer to accepting that reality.

The two hounds were dangerously close, the sight of their internal organs hanging out of their body too close for comfort. Sophia took her own advice and closed her eyes.

She knew there were dangers in the world. There always would be, but she was safe and secure with the creature she was holding onto. She was safe as long as she quit running from danger and faced it head-on. Sometimes that meant fighting, and sometimes it meant simply facing what she feared.

When she was close to falling asleep, Sophia opened her eyes to find the dingoes almost nose to nose with her. She should have jumped to her feet and defended herself. Instead, she hugged her dragon, opened her mouth, and said, "Welcome to our humble abode. Enjoy your stay."

And with that, the rider and her dragon fell asleep, hoping the strangest magic they'd ever used worked.

CHAPTER TWENTY-SIX

The dreams Sophia had that night were strange, yet they made her feel invigorated when she woke. Maybe it was simply the fact she woke up at all, which made her feel inspired.

Lunis stirred at the same time as her, just before sunrise, to find their camp empty. They were still in one piece, not a single mark on them from the zombie dingoes.

Sophia pushed up as the reality started to dawn on her. It was hard to believe it had worked.

We didn't fight, and we survived, Lunis declared, his voice clouded with disbelief.

"I think there's a beautiful lesson here," she stated, surveying their camp, which needed a lot of attention.

It's a beautiful Sophism, Lunis said, affectionately.

"Sophism?" she questioned.

Yes, things Sophia says and does that should be in a book.

"Or on a t-shirt?" she teased.

He batted his eyes at her, looking much more energized than the days prior. *My dragon proverbs go on t-shirts. Your stuff needs to be in libraries. Maybe even put on GIFs.*

Sophia laughed. "Oh, wow, I've gotten big enough for GIFs. What's next? Memes?"

Don't go crazy just yet, he joked. *But in all seriousness, you're the queen at knowing when to fight and when to stand down. The dingoes, we could have fought to the death. We could have defended ourselves every single night. But you pieced it all together and realized we didn't have to fight. That fighting only encouraged them. When we stayed still and gave them no reaction, they moved on, bored without any attention. I feel like the same thing happens in life all the time. You react to someone and it incites them. You ignore them and they go away.*

Sophia smiled, realizing how accurate his words were. "Yes, most people are zombie dingoes, aren't they?"

Yes, he affirmed. *And most try to fight them. Few have the good sense to close their eyes when a drooling monster is in their face threatening them. You knew to invite in your demons, and that was what saved us.*

Sophia let out a heavy breath, wondering if they had come full circle yet. She wasn't sure. They still had a few more days in the Australian Outback, which shouldn't be underestimated. "Well, you did catch our dinner for the last few days, which I think saved us."

Lunis gave her a meaningful expression. *Sophia, we saved each other. That's the way. The way it is now and for all time. You and I are nothing without one another.*

Sophia was skinnier than she ever remembered. She was dirty in every place possible. There were smells about her she wasn't sure would ever go away, yet she felt stronger and better than ever before.

Somehow by being broken down, she had found a part of her she absolutely adored. A part that complemented her dragon in ways neither had realized.

Sophia and Lunis still had much to learn about the world and each other. There was so much to discover. So many things to do and be. But right then, the pair felt completely bonded to one another and to the world they were trying to understand. One day they would save it, although neither knew that was going to be their destiny.

CHAPTER TWENTY-SEVEN

It only took a day for Sophia and Lunis to find a routine that suited them. She spent the morning caring for the shelter, which didn't take long to repair.

The dragon hunted for them while she collected water. Later they ate, listening to the Outback and discussing things that were unique for them. They talked about ideas and philosophies, rambling on for hours about things neither had ever considered. Sophia found that whereas before she missed Wilder, Mahkah, Ainsley, Quiet, and maybe even Hiker and Evan, she didn't feel that way anymore. She felt fulfilled within in a new way.

When night began to fall, they both tensed briefly before remembering they weren't there to fight the Outback.

"We are here to be one with it," Sophia reminded. "We are here to be one with ourselves."

Lunis nodded. Doing as he had the nights prior, he curled up and made a space for Sophia.

The zombie dingoes returned every night and made their presence known. The pair got better at ignoring them. Not really ignoring. If one ignores their demons, they slowly take over.

Instead, the two just quit giving their power away to the monsters.

They rested at night. They thought sweet thoughts. They prepared for the day ahead instead of giving everything away to the demons who would inevitably slay them with exhaustion if given the opportunity.

On the final day in the Australian Outback, Sophia rose, feeling more energized than when she had plumbing and the Castle provided everything for her. She wasn't sure why, since she hadn't had a proper shower or meal in a week. But somehow in the Outback, she'd found her own brand of magic and mixed it with Lunis' they'd managed just fine. She ventured to say they were thriving.

She didn't look much like before. Her pants had been altered to be shorts since she'd lost the one pant leg on the first day. Her shirt had been torn so many times she had pulled off the sleeves and repurposed parts of the fabric into bits she'd wrapped around her arms and wrists. She personified the look of a strange tribal warrior.

Her hair was a gigantic mess, as Lunis liked to remind her. However, she'd found a way to corral it back into a strange assortment of dread-like braids. Her face was covered in dirt most of the time, although she tried to take a proper bath in the lake most mornings.

Often, she hoped to see Smeg again, but the croc didn't surface. She suspected he'd moved on to a different body of water somewhere on the Earth and hoped to find him again in the future. He was helpful in his own crazy way.

Since they hadn't had to spend their time battling any more rabid dogs or giant spiders, the two had taken up hobbies. Sophia had started to make jewelry out of the stones she'd collected. Around her wrists and neck, she wore several bracelets and necklaces fashioned from homemade rope.

More surprisingly, Lunis had started painting, although

Sophia had hoped he'd take up baking. Alas, he said that would be impossible since he didn't know how to come by any leavening ingredients in the Outback.

He had created beautiful paintings on the wall by their shelter using the clay from the lake and coloring it with dyes from wildflowers. The paintings were masterpieces Sophia had never seen in real life, complete with pictures of Scotland and Los Angeles and her travels. It was at nightfall on their last day she realized why she couldn't pull her eyes from the paintings.

"You created our life," she whispered to her dragon.

I immortalized it, he said. *But yes. It only seemed fitting since we were on this soul journey.*

"I like our life," Sophia said.

I think that was the point to all this, Lunis said. *If you came out of this not liking where you came from, you'd probably be stuck here until you figured out how to change it. But you like where we came from, and I daresay you want to go back, don't you?*

She turned, smiling wide at Lunis. "With all my heart. But what I realized more than anything is that no matter where I call home, which presently and hopefully forever is the Castle, I only ever want to be somewhere if you are too. I really thought growing up in the House of Fourteen was my home. And then my place with Liv. And later, the Castle. But now…after the Outback, I know the truth." Sophia reached out and stroked her dragon's face. "You are my home. Where you are, no matter if the conditions are pleasant or hellish, I want to be there. No matter what."

One hundred percent, Lunis said.

And as if prompted by their words, a portal opened beside them, sent by the Castle to bring them back to the real world, where there were real problems that needed their help now that they were aligned.

CHAPTER TWENTY-EIGHT

The cold of the Expanse was such a contrast to the Australian Outback that Sophia slipped on her cloak first thing after stepping through the portal.

She drank in the fresh, clean air, enjoying how it instantly seemed to refresh her. The green of the hills was such a contrast to the red dirt and muted colors of the Outback it almost hurt Sophia's eyes.

The sight of the three dragonriders waiting for her just outside the Barrier was definitely welcomed. Sophia found herself rushing in their direction, realizing how much she'd missed them—even Evan.

Evan offered her a repulsed expression as she approached and reeled backward. Mahkah stood stoically, his hands pinned behind his back. Wilder had his arms extended, welcoming Sophia with a hug, relief evident in his blue eyes.

When she was close enough, he dropped his arms and leaned back, squinting at her with disbelief. "Wow, that's a new look for you."

Sophia glanced down at her ripped clothes, covered in dirt and grime. The armored shirt, once light-colored, was almost black. Sophia's nails were caked in mud. It would take Mae Ling…well, no time at all to clean them up, but Sophia would need to stop by and see her fairy godmother soon. She knew her hair looked like it belonged on a hippie, arranged into thick dreadlocks down her back.

Evan covered his nose. "Dude, which one of you smells?" he asked Sophia and Lunis.

"I took a bath this morning," Sophia replied. "Lun hasn't had one all week."

It's her, Lunis argued. *She took a bath in swamp water.* He glanced affectionately at Sophia. *There was a reason I didn't bathe.*

"I thought it was because you were pretending to be one of these guys," she joked.

"Welcome back," Mahkah said, bowing respectfully.

Wilder held out a single hand and went to slap Sophia on the shoulder but pulled it back just before connecting with her. "Yeah, welcome back."

"So, you didn't die?" Evan asked, his nose still covered.

"You're still here so wishing on those Outback stars didn't work," she teased, winking at him.

"You will have to tell us all about it," Wilder said, looking Lunis over.

"Yeah, let's start with what did you do to your dragon?" Evan asked, also inspecting him.

"I adorned him with jewelry," Sophia said proudly. Her dragon had her handmade necklaces arranged on his head like a crown. There were a few wrapped around his neck and legs, the shiny gems winking in the light.

She pulled a few bracelets from the pocket of her cloak and handed them out. "I made ones for each of you, too."

Evan gave his bracelet back and shook his head. "I'm good. I don't wear anything that reminds me of the Outback."

Wilder, however, slipped his on and tightened it on his wrist. "That's just because you were nearly eaten by a talking crocodile."

Sophia gave Evan a surprised expression. "Smeg tried to eat you? Oh, he was super helpful to me."

Evan sighed. "Of course, he was. Please tell me the zombie dingoes did try to eat you."

Sophia laughed. "You're so thoughtful. Who needs enemies when I've got you? And yes, the dingoes tried to eat us."

Evan punched the air. "Yes!"

Lunis lowered his head and looked at the giddy rider. *Well, until Sophia realized not to fight them, and they left us alone.*

Sophia stretched. "Then we got some proper rest."

The wide smile on Evan's face disappeared. "You what?"

"You didn't fight the dingoes?" Mahkah asked, intrigued.

"Yeah, would it have been cheating to tell us we'd encounter rabid zombie dogs?" Sophia asked, her hands on her hips.

"I'm afraid it would have been," Mahkah answered. "But again, you didn't fight them?"

No, we invited them into our house, so to speak, Lunis said, seeming much lighter as his head floated around, the necklaces making him look like a hippie too.

"W-wh-what?" Wilder asked. "You had a house?"

Sophia shrugged. "No, not really. Just a roof, but metaphorically speaking, we invited our houseguests in and welcomed them."

"They didn't chew off your faces?" Evan asked, his mouth wide and his eyes bulging.

"They totally did. This is my new face." Sophia shook her head.

"Well, it's dirty," Evan replied. "Have you looked in a mirror? And I think you have a bush in your hair. Oh, and have I mentioned you smell bad?"

"She smells rugged," Wilder corrected. "Like a cowboy or a girl who has spent a week in the Australian Outback."

"The zombie dingoes," Mahkah said, bringing the conversation back to the topic. "You really didn't fight them?"

"Well, we did for a couple of nights," Sophia explained. "However, it was going to be exhausting if we kept it up. It was a losing battle—"

"Which is the charm of the trip," Evan stated, crossing his arms and looking bitter about the whole thing.

Sophia shook her head. "Then I had the idea that we wouldn't defend ourselves. It seemed the more we fought, the more excited they got. When we started to ignore them, they became less interested and eventually left us alone."

Mahkah combed his fingers over his chin. "Interesting. A risk but a strategic one."

Wilder shook his head, astonished. "Simi and I fought those dingoes for seven days, sleeping during the day, and you simply closed your eyes and ignored them?"

She nodded proudly.

"I lived in a tree," Evan said, disgusted.

"I killed all the spiders under that tree," Sophia said.

"Well, you two obviously bonded," Mahkah said, looking at her and Lunis. "You completed all the objectives of the training exercise."

The group turned for the Castle, crossing the boundary to the Gullington and striding in time with one another. Lunis set off for the Cave when they crossed the Barrier. The Castle was a welcome sight in the distance. Sophia could already smell scones and couldn't wait to slip into clean clothes after a long hot shower.

"But the question is, did you have fun?" Wilder asked, a crooked smile on his face.

A week ago, Sophia would have scowled at the question. Now, she found herself nodding. "I wouldn't have called any of it fun, but rewarding, absolutely."

Evan's eyes were directed at the grass under their feet as he shook his head. "She didn't fight the dingoes. Dude, that's not fair."

Wilder slapped him on the back with a laugh. "It's a good lesson for us."

"Yes," Mahkah said, meditating on an idea. "Sometimes, we fight. Sometimes we ignore evil. It's knowing when to act and when not to."

The guys halted in front of the Castle, their cool demeanors suddenly fading and serious expressions taking over their faces. Sensing a new tension, Sophia looked at them.

"What is it?" she asked.

"Someone evil has surfaced since you two left," Wilder explained. "Thad Reinhart."

"Oh," Sophia said with relief. "We know about him."

"Yeah, but he's accelerated his agenda," Mahkah explained. "Hiker will want to see you."

"As soon as you wash that nappy hair," Evan added.

Sophia nodded. "Okay. I'll go straight to his office once I'm clean."

All the excitement from returning faded as worry took over. The expressions on the guys' faces told her that whatever had happened while they were gone wasn't just mildly bad. She got the impression it was catastrophic.

"And remember to wash behind…well, your everything," Evan called as she hurried up the stairs and into the Castle. "Wash twice."

CHAPTER TWENTY-NINE

I t took more like five washings to feel clean. The brush nearly broke when Sophia tried to pull it through her locks. She considered keeping the dreadlocks, which Evan had had before he got electrocuted and all his hair was fried off. The thought that Evan had once sported the same hairdo was enough to make her work through the tangles, returning her hair to its usual sleek appearance.

When Sophia exited the bathroom, she was pleasantly surprised to find Ainsley tending the fire in her room. She'd also set down tea and scones for Sophia as if she'd read her mind about what she was craving.

"The Castle told me while you were showering you *needed* scones," Ainsley explained, rising from the fireplace and brushing off her hands on her apron. "Need seemed a bit of an exaggeration, but that's typical of the Castle."

Sophia realized how happy she was to see the housekeeper when she threw her arms around her and hugged her.

Ainsley tensed, her arms stick straight by her side. "S. Beaufont?"

"Yes?" Sophia asked, hugging Ainsley tightly.

"What are you doing?"

Sophia pulled away. "I was hugging you."

"Yes, but we're not hugging types around here," she said, taking a sudden step backward. "And you and I aren't really on those terms."

Sophia waved her off and took a seat away from the fire, having had enough warmth for ages. She picked up a scone, looking forward to her first refreshments since returning.

"Did you have a good time on holiday?" Ainsley asked, pouring her a cup of tea.

Sophia shook her head. "I was on a walkabout in the Australian Outback."

"Same thing," Ainsley said, standing back and looking Sophia over. "You lost weight. And you're sunburned. What are all those scratches on your arms from?"

Sophia glanced at the various marks on her skin. "Revolting spiders. If I never see one again, it will be too soon."

"Do you want me to clear out the family who lives under your bed then?" Ainsley asked.

She'd made that joke before, but Sophia was starting to wonder if it was a joke. Taking a bite of the scone, she relished its sweetness, perfectly crumbly and dense, as it melted in her mouth.

"I'd sure like to take a holiday like you all get regularly," Ainsley said, plopping down on the seat next to Sophia and putting her boots up on the coffee table. "I haven't left the Castle to do anything but go to town for supplies in ages."

Sophia nearly choked on her bite. She was one of the few who knew Ainsley couldn't leave the Castle for long or she'd fall victim to the curse Thad Reinhart had put on her, the one meant to kill Hiker. It had stolen her memory, changed her life, and given her the scar on the side of her head.

Sophia believed there had to be a way to change things, but right then wasn't the time to investigate. She wanted to take her time sipping tea and chewing on scones, but instead, she gulped down her tea and hardly chewed. Something was going on with Thad and his evil plans, and Sophia knew she needed to report to Hiker right away.

"The Castle missed you," Ainsley said, grabbing a scone and spreading clotted cream and jam on it.

"It did?" Sophia asked, perking up. "How do you know?"

"Because it told me," Ainsley answered. "It made portraits of you and Looney."

Sophia giggled. "That's a good nickname for him. I'm sure he'll hate it."

"Good," Ainsley chirped. "I'll be sure to use it and never call him anything else."

"The Castle and you," Sophia began, carefully. "You seem to understand it better these days, is that right?"

Ainsley tilted her head back and forth undecidedly. "I understand it when it wants me to. Sometimes the messages are clear, and other times they are just hints. It really depends on its mood. It was quite sour while you were gone. I had to do most of the chores twice since it seemed it wanted to be dirty in your absence."

Sophia laughed and took a bite of a cream cheese and cucumber sandwich. Somehow it was the best thing she'd ever put in her mouth. "It must have wanted to be just like me when I was in the Outback."

"The boys missed you too, although they wouldn't admit it," Ainsley offered. "Meals were incredibly boring. They kept looking around like they were expecting you to pop in late, wearing something colorful and humming one of your pop songs."

"That's nice to hear," Sophia said, smiling at the idea.

"You've changed a lot around the Castle since you showed up," Ainsley said. "Quiet says the biggest change is yet to come. Once you complete your training, he says."

"What?" Sophia lowered the sandwich and blinked at the housekeeper. "What does he mean?"

She shrugged. "Who knows, but he's never been wrong."

"And you understand him too," Sophia stated. "How is that?"

"I don't know why you people can't understand him," Ainsley said. "He's as plain as day to me."

There was weird magic surrounding the groundskeeper. Sophia had understood him a time or two, the first occasion being when he helped her. Then he'd promised her, if she stuck around, he'd tell her his real name. She was still hoping he made good on the promise because it was of great curiosity to her.

"Ains?" Sophia asked after a brief moment of silence. It had never been a big deal for her, but now she was much more comfortable when it got quiet. "If you could go anywhere in the world, where would you like to go?"

The housekeeper chewed, thinking. "I'm not sure. Honestly, I don't even know why I don't just leave here and go on a walkabout. It's just that every time I consider traveling, I quickly lose interest."

Sophia nodded, knowing the Castle was behind the brainwashing, trying to keep Ainsley safe and alive, although the inevitable result was, she was sheltered.

"I guess I'd like to see a beach," Ainsley said after a moment of consideration. "It's been ages since I've seen the ocean and a cabana boy serving me drinks while I wiggle my toes in the sand seems just about like the best thing ever. Then I can say something really awful like, 'Life's a beach and then you dive.'"

Smiling, Sophia stretched to a standing position. "Well, I hope you get your beach vacation. Maybe Quiet will even join you."

"Oh, S. Beaufont," Ainsley scolded, sitting forward. "I don't leave the Gullington often because…well, I don't know why. There isn't any real need, I guess. But Quiet? He can't for hardly more than a few minutes."

"He can't?" Sophia asked. "Why not?"

Ainsley's expression changed. "You don't know? Of course, you don't know. Anyway, I've said too much."

"No, Ains," Sophia argued as the housekeeper busied herself picking up the tray and hurrying for the door. "Why can't Quiet leave the Gullington for long? I won't tell anyone."

"Pretend I didn't say anything," Ainsley said, the door automatically opening for her since her hands were full of the tray. "Now, you better be off. Hiker will be disappointed you survived, and I'm looking forward to hearing his grumbling on the matter. So off you go."

Sophia simply nodded and watched as the housekeeper sped out of the room. There were always more mysteries to the Gullington, waiting to be unraveled.

CHAPTER THIRTY

The portrait of Sophia and Lunis was quite nice, she observed on her way to Hiker's office. It was a sizable painting, about two by four feet. The pair were standing in front of the Pond, the sunlight shimmering over the water as Sophia stood next to her dragon, one of her arms resting on his back.

"I missed you too," Sophia said aloud to the Castle.

The flames in the sconces lengthened in response.

"Are you going to tell me why Quiet can't leave the Gullington?"

There was no visible response from the Castle.

"Okay. Are you going to lead me on a scavenger hunt so I can discover the secret on my own?" she asked.

Again, the Castle didn't seem interested in providing any answers.

Sophia sighed as she headed for Hiker's office.

It was strange to see Hiker's study the way it was the first time she saw it. All of his books lined the shelves, and the Elite Globe was back in its place next to the bank of windows. The furniture looked great in the space and had plenty of room around it, unlike when the Castle had shrunk the area to a fraction of the size to punish Hiker for his secret-keeping.

The one thing different from before were newspapers from all over the world, written in different languages, lying all over the place. Even stranger were several television screens stationed around the office, all broadcasting news reports.

"I saw you were back," Hiker said, indicating the Elite Globe when Sophia ducked her head into the room.

Mama Jamba had a bunch of wadded-up tissues littering the sofa around her. The woman's nose was red, and her eyes were swollen from crying.

"Mama Jamba, are you okay?" Sophia asked, rushing over and taking the old woman's hand at once. She worried whatever Thad Reinhart had done was too far gone to stop. Was the Earth in total peril? Was it too late? Was this the end?

Mama Jamba sniffed and squeezed Sophia's hand. "Yeah, I'm fine. I just got finished watching *The Notebook*, and it still has me all emotional."

"What?" Sophia asked, not expecting that answer. "You mean, Nicholas Sparks' movie?"

Mama Jamba nodded and grabbed another tissue to dry her eyes.

"I told you these screens were for monitoring world events, not for watching that sappy stuff," Hiker said with authority.

Mama Jamba pointed to one of the televisions broadcasting a female reporter holding a microphone, standing in front of a picketing crowd. The screen changed to show the beginning of the *City of Angels* movie. "I'm in the mood to watch sad and depressing movies. Sue me. My Earth is in danger, and this is how I'm going to deal with it."

Sophia glanced at Hiker, a questioning expression on her face. He simply shrugged in reply.

"What's going on?" Sophia asked, looking at the two.

"Well," Mama Jamba began, wiping her nose. "There's this

doctor, and she tries to save lives. That's Meg Ryan's character. And Nicholas Cage is an angel. Not like the ones who created the dragonriders. Fictional angels."

"Mama," Hiker interrupted, "I believe Sophia meant, what's going on in the world, not the synopsis for that drivel you're watching."

"Oh, well, then I won't spoil it for you, but you all talk quietly," Mama Jamba urged. "I'm going to watch this film and cry."

Sophia rose from the couch and shot the strange woman a questioning expression. "Hiker, is everything okay?"

He shook his head. "We'll get to that. Anyway, you returned from the Outback. Good on you. Not so hard, was it?"

Sophia eyed her fingernails, which were still not as clean as she would have liked. "I survived."

"And the dingoes?" he asked. "Did they take a toe?"

"She didn't fight the dingoes because she's smarter than the lot of you," Mama Jamba said, taking a bite out of a chocolate truffle. Sophia didn't remember seeing those there a moment ago.

"She what?" Hiker questioned. "Of course, she did."

"For two days she did, but then she figured it out," Mama Jamba said, her focus on the television screen in front of her. Briefly, she pulled her gaze away and looked at Sophia. "You're a smart one. That's how I know you'll finish training in record time. If you don't, well, we're all going to hell anyway at this rate."

Sophia had many questions, but before she could voice them, Hiker interrupted her thoughts. He apparently had his own questions.

"What does she mean?" he asked, pointing at Mama Jamba. "You didn't fight the dingoes?"

"They just wanted to fight," Sophia explained and gave him the full story.

When she was done, he stroked his beard, a skeptical glint in his blue eyes. "That's an interesting approach. It could have backfired completely."

"It's called faith, my dear. If more had it, I wouldn't be perishing," Mama Jamba chimed in, her attention still on the television as she finished another truffle. It was like she wasn't listening, yet she responded in time.

Hiker rolled his eyes. "Would you stop being so melodramatic, Mama? You aren't going anywhere, and neither is your Earth. I'll see to that, especially now that Sophia is back."

"Her training, Hiker," Mama Jamba sang. Her Southern accent made the words sound soft, even though they were filled with demand.

"Thad has taken a serious advantage," Hiker argued, leaning across his desk and staring at the woman who was staring at the television as Meg Ryan delivered a speech.

"Which is why she's going to progress with her training," Mama Jamba said, holding out her hand, an Old-Fashioned materializing in her fingers. She smiled at it, although the gesture was marked by a tender hurt in her eyes. The old woman took a sip and then wiped her mouth. "Oh, that hits the spot. No one makes an Old-Fashioned quite like you, Castle."

"If we could focus for a moment, it would be wise," Hiker said, irritation in his voice.

Mama Jamba waved him on. "Go on then. I'll cut in when I see fit. But right now, it's getting to the good part, so y'all keep it down."

Hiker sighed and returned his attention to Sophia. "While you were gone, Thad accelerated his plans. I believe he's been working on them for quite some time. Maybe he wasn't planning on moving ahead like this quite yet—"

"He wasn't," Mama Jamba cut in, sipping her drink.

Hiker nodded, obviously annoyed at being interrupted. "Anyway, I'm guessing our presence has worried him, so he's taking action. I didn't realize how much control and power he has. His hands are in every part of the international government. He has corporations all over the world that contribute to widespread problems. He's instigating discord all over the globe." Hiker threw his hand at the many newspapers littering his desk. "I should have seen it coming. I should have known how powerful he was."

"Why didn't you?" Sophia asked, and instantly regretted it based on the scolding look he shot her.

"It's a good question," Mama Jamba said, coming to her defense. "You need to explain yourself, Hiker."

He obviously wasn't used to being ordered around by two women, one who questioned him and the other who made demands. After a moment, he said, "Thad and I used to be connected. I told you I worked to block him. Well, since I admitted he wasn't gone from this Earth, I've tried to find him." He pointed to the Elite Globe. "I tried to track him down, but he isn't one of us anymore, and he doesn't have a dragon, so my methods haven't worked. And I believe he's used magitech to block me now."

"Okay, that makes sense," Sophia said.

"Anyway, Thad is much more powerful and far-reaching than I envisioned," Hiker continued. "He's on the brink of instigating a war among strong countries who have devastating capabilities. They can't see they're going to destroy each other to settle their disputes, so I have to assume he's using magic to brainwash them."

"And money," Mama Jamba added. "Money is magic on the mind. It will make perfectly good humans do imperfect things."

Hiker nodded. "However he's done it, the ball is in motion, and it will result in a war."

"So that's what you're doing?" Sophia asked, pointing at the various televisions. "You're monitoring what's happening around the world based on Thad's plans?"

Hiker nodded and growled at the same time. "I didn't like

bringing technology into the Castle, but you'd already done it, and I guess it was overdue. Anyway, I defaulted to the most practical solution. I need information, and I need it fast to deal with things."

Sophia wanted to congratulate him on the big step into the twenty-first century, but it seemed ill-timed. She'd wait until he was more used to having technology around since he was presently scowling at the closest television screen. That also might have been because it was showing a report about how neighboring countries were hours from a seemingly unstoppable war.

"Now that you're back," Hiker continued, "I want you and the other men—"

"Riders," Mama Jamba corrected, now chomping on popcorn.

Sophia had no idea where that had come from either, much like the chocolate and drink.

"The other riders are men," Hiker spat. "I think I can get away with saying it that way."

"I just think it would be better if you adopted more inclusive speech when referring to your riders," Mama Jamba chimed.

"Anyway, as I was saying, now that you're back—"

"She's got training to attend to," Mama Jamba interrupted.

Hiker sighed. "It will have to wait."

"It really can't," Mama Jamba argued.

"Well, we need all the riders intervening on these issues," Hiker declared. "Chaos is breaking out everywhere. If we aren't adjudicating, then Thad is going to—"

"Oh, he's going to regardless," Mama Jamba cut in. "He's too far ahead."

Hiker threw up his hands in frustration. "Thanks for the vote of confidence."

She waved him off, still watching the television. "This is your own fault for putting your head in the sand all those years. But it's not all lost. You just have to ensure you show up at the right time with the ammo. More importantly, you have to ensure you show up to the final battle as the right person. That's more crucial than the time and the place and everything that's happened before."

Hiker shook his head. "I don't know what you're talking about, Mama."

"I get that," Mama Jamba agreed, shoveling popcorn into her mouth. "Anyway, send the other riders on these adjudicator missions, but Sophia has to finish training. They can keep things at bay until we're ready for the war."

Hiker stood, his actions abrupt. He was vibrating with tension. "I don't want a war."

Mama Jamba glanced up at him. "I get that, son. But it's too late for that. You've let this go on too long. War is inevitable. Now it's just a matter of when and what you and your riders will bring when it happens."

"Mama," he began.

"Hiker, the war of the brothers was forecast by Papa Creola long ago," she said, her voice hoarse from crying. "I've known that. Now it's time you do too. And there's something else."

"What?" Hiker gave her a long cold stare.

"A good part is coming up," Mama Jamba answered, returning her focus to the screen and shushing Hiker.

He shook his head, frustrated by the woman. "Anyway, go finish your training, Sophia. When the time comes for war, you'll need to be ready. When I have to take Thad down, I'll need you prepared."

"Thing about that, Hiker," Mama Jamba cut in again, throwing a piece of popcorn into the air and catching it expertly in her mouth.

He turned his head to the side and gave her an impatient glare. "What?"

"Well, if we're being candid with one another—"

"We aren't," he cut in.

"Of course, we are," she disagreed. "Anyway, the thing is

you're not in a position to face your brother right now, and I think we all know that."

"What are you talking about, Mama?" he asked, shaking his head at her.

"Oh, come on, dear. You know you lost your confidence," Mama Jamba said, pointing her finger at the screen and making her movie pause. "It's a good part. Can't miss this for you all."

"No, you wouldn't want to miss some Hollywood movie for the war efforts brewing on your planet," Hiker said, his voice dripping with condescension.

"No, I wouldn't," Mama Jamba agreed with a nod, not catching his sarcasm. "Anyway, it shouldn't be news to you that Thad has gotten fresh skills while you've been chronicling the monotonous events at the Gullington." She indicated the logbook on the corner of Hiker's desk.

He grimaced at the book and shook his head. "I have skills."

"He is aware of the modern world where you have refused even to acknowledge much has changed in the last few centuries," Mama Jamba continued.

"I have televisions in here, don't I?" he claimed.

"At my behest," she stated. "The final battle will inevitably be you and your brother, Hiker. Your riders have to get you there, but once they do, you'll be on your own, as you've often sent them on their own with only their training and their dragon for assistance."

"What's your point, Mama?" he asked, sounding weary.

"My point is, if you're going to face your twin, you have to bone up on your training," she declared.

He scoffed. "I'm as strong as I was four centuries ago when I magnetized to Bell."

She shook her head. "You're missing the point. I know you've been out on the Expanse practicing combat and lifting weights for centuries. You're strong. There's no doubt about it. And you know how to ride your dragon better than anyone. However, what you've lost over the years was the most crucial part of training for any in the Dragon Elite."

She was quiet for a moment.

Sophia glanced between Hiker and Mama Jamba, wondering which person would speak next. They seemed to be facing off, a staring contest between the two.

After a long pause, Hiker said, "What do you mean?"

"I mean, you need a refresher in training," she stated.

"I don't either!" he revolted.

"You also need an attitude adjustment," she fired back.

"A week in the Australian Outback might fix that," Sophia offered.

Hiker rolled his eyes.

Mama Jamba smiled and winked at her. "Good call, darling, but I think I have a better idea."

"What are you cooking up, Mama?" Hiker asked in a low voice.

"You've lost the connection with yourself," she stated.

"I have not!" he protested.

"Don't argue with me," she said, sounding tired all of a sudden. "Of course, you have. When have you needed to feel the intuition in your spirit? Not when you had no missions because the Dragon Elite were effectively useless for a few centuries. When have you needed to connect to the Earth? Not while you were hiding in the Gullington pretending you were useless."

"Mama," he began.

She held up her hand, pausing him. "Hiker, I love you more than anyone, but it's time I wake you up from this dream you're in. Thad is back."

"I know that!" he boomed.

"And you think you're enough to face him when the time comes," she fired back.

"I'm the only one who can face him," Hiker argued.

"I agree, dear," she said in a much quieter voice. "Nevertheless, you aren't even remotely in the right place for such things."

"What are you proposing?" he asked.

She lowered her chin, a mischievous expression in her eyes. "You know what the next part of Sophia's training includes."

"No," he said with a growl, his chin low to his chest and his eyes full of heat.

"Oh, yes, my dear," Mama Jamba answered.

"You don't mean..." Hiker trailed away, sounding almost as mad as Sophia had ever heard him.

"I absolutely do," Mama Jamba answered.

"But..."

"Oh yes," she answered in reply to the question he left hanging.

"I need to be here," Hiker reasoned.

"You need to do everything possible to win this war," she said.

"But the news reports." Hiker lifted his hand to indicate the closest television screen.

"You need to be ready for what's coming that only you can fight," Mama Jamba stated.

"And the men?" Hiker asked. Receiving a scolding expression from Mama Jamba, he shook his head. "I mean, the other riders? Who will give them their orders?"

Mama Jamba waved him off. "This isn't forever, Hiker. This is just a training exercise. Assign your riders and then go off on your own. You'll be back before you know it and better than ever. That's the hope anyway."

Hiker let out a long furious breath before starting for the door. "Come on, Sophia."

She gave Mama Jamba a questioning expression.

"Go on, my dear," Mother Nature encouraged, urging Sophia to follow the leader of the Dragon Elite.

"But..."

"But nothing," Hiker ordered. "Follow me. We have training to get to."

"I don't understand," Sophia said, taking tentative steps.

He turned at the threshold to the door and gave Mama Jamba a frustrated expression. "Nor do I. But the person I take orders from is never wrong. And she seems to think the next part of your training needs to commence, and I need to join you for it."

CHAPTER THIRTY-ONE

Sophia had to run to keep up with Hiker as he strode down the stairs to the first floor.

"Sir, what do you mean?" Sophia asked Hiker's retreating back.

He turned, letting out an impatient sigh. "I mean, I've been sent back to school by the one person I'm not allowed to refuse."

"You mean Mama?" she asked, pointing over her shoulder. Putting it all together, she sighed with a sudden realization. "Oh, so you have to take the training with me. Oh, wow, that's got to be…"

Sophia's voice trailed off based on the murderous expression on Hiker's face.

"Right," he growled angrily. "We need to journey off to the far side of the Expanse, past where you've been before to reach the far side of the Barrier on the edge of the Pond. Once we're there, we're outside of the conscious protection of the Castle and we can hear our internal voices, so—"

"Excuse me, sir," Sophia interrupted. "I'm sorry to stop you, but I have zero idea what you're talking about."

He nodded and let out another audible sigh. "I need you to go stock up supplies for a training exercise that will start first thing at sunrise tomorrow morning."

"With you, sir?" she questioned.

He nodded.

"And I get to bring things?" she asked. "Unlike in the Outback?"

"You get to bring food and water," he answered. "No electronics."

"We'll be gone for how long?" she asked.

"For as long as it takes," he replied.

"Well, since you've done this before, I was hoping you could fill me in."

"Why?" he asked, totally put off by the questions. "Do you have an engagement to attend?"

"Well, there are some babies being born I promised—" The impatient expression on Hiker's face cut her off. "You know what? I have all the time in the world. Well, until your twin brother ends it and then I'm busy shoveling coal in hell for the rest of eternity."

He glanced at the ceiling. "If nothing else, angels, please use this training to stifle her attempts at humor."

"So, I should meet you where and when for this lovely excursion?" Sophia asked.

He pointed to where they stood at the entrance to the Castle. "Be here first thing tomorrow morning. We leave then, and we won't be back until we're done."

Sophia nodded, recognizing asking for more information would only incite the man more. She was about to set off on a training excursion for an unknown amount of time with someone she followed and respected but couldn't stand. Worst of all, she was certain that too much time with her might drive Hiker Wallace to the brink of insanity. She wasn't sure he'd be safe to be around at that point.

Sophia wondered if this was the point of the training exercise.

Only one way to find out.

CHAPTER THIRTY-TWO

Sophia met Hiker at the front of the Castle at sunrise, as she was told. She'd brought a bag of food and a canteen of water. Holding it up, she shook it at his face. "I'm ready."

He grabbed the bag, pulled it out of her grasp, and threw it across the entrance hall. "And now you're not."

Sophia didn't tense. Instead, she glanced over her shoulder to where her food and water had exploded against the wall. "Did I mishear the whole 'bring whatever you like' stuff?"

He shook his head. "But this is life, Sophia. Sometimes you're told you get reparation, and then the world goes back on it."

"Are we still talking about our training and you and me?" she asked tentatively.

"Mostly…not really," he said with a new bitterness in his eyes.

She pointed over her shoulder to where her supplies were. "So I can't get that?"

He shook his head. "I've changed my mind. No supplies. We won't be gone long. You just have to concentrate and make this the shortest possible long part of the training."

Hiker turned and walked out of the Castle, his chin high.

Sophia hurried after him, the cold air of the Expanse making her suck in a sudden breath.

"Did you just insinuate that this is the longest part of the training, sir?" Sophia asked, running to catch up with the Viking, whose strides were three times the length of hers.

He kept moving forward as he spoke. "It depends. Some riders take several months to finish this phase."

"Oh, hell…" Sophia said, halting and looking back to the Castle, considering going back for her food and water.

"And others have passed in only a short period of time," Hiker continued.

"Short period of time?" she questioned, not having moved even though Hiker continued to move in the direction of the Pond.

"It all depends on you, Sophia."

"Like seven days in the Australian Outback?" she asked. "Or like three days in the Sahara? Or like a month in Texas? Can you give me an idea here?"

"Follow me," he urged. "You don't need supplies."

She hesitated, really wanting to go back for her supplies. She didn't like the idea of once again being unprepared. When Hiker disappeared around the other side of the Castle, she sped after him, not wanting him to get out of sight. Yes, it was intimidating to go on an excursion with Hiker Wallace, but it was also a great honor. He might not think of her as his favorite rider, but that didn't mean Sophia didn't relish the time with him. For as many conflicts as the two had, she respected him greatly. She wanted him to like her. She wanted to like him. Maybe this was that opportunity.

"Are you sure I won't need supplies?" Sophia asked, sprinting to catch up with him. "Is it because I can use magic? I mean—"

"I'm certain of it," he answered, continuing to make for the Pond.

"Oh, well, can you explain, sir?" she asked, finally catching up properly. "You think we won't be out here long? Is it because you've already passed this training once?"

"That's part of it," he said, halting when they reached the water's edge and looking around as if searching for something.

"What's the other part?" she asked, wondering what he was looking for.

He gazed down at her with pure annoyance. "It's you, Sophia."

She felt like he'd just pointed an accusatory finger at her. "Me? What about me?"

"We won't be out here long because of you," he stated bitterly.

"Did I do something wrong, sir?" she asked.

He shook his head. "No, that's just the thing. It took Evan twelve weeks to pass this portion of the training. Wilder was out here for a blistering week. Mahkah, well, he's him, so only a few days. And Adam, well…" He chuckled at a long-ago memory. "The bloke never told me honestly how long this part of the training took him, but he hinted it was only a few hours, and you are more like Adam than anyone I've yet to meet…but I also don't get out much."

Sophia fumbled for words. "I don't understand what you're trying to tell me, sir."

Hiker licked his fingertips and held them out to the blistering wind that rolled across the Expanse.

He turned, not at all appearing to be a fun travel partner. "I'm saying I expect you, Sophia Beaufont, to do what you usually do."

Sophia blinked at him blankly. "Be a total pain in your ass and oppose everything you ask or demand?"

He shook his head. "No. Well, yes, I do expect that from you. I was just saying that similar to your excursion in the Outback, I expect you to pass through this one with exemplary marks, faster than most. You are Sophia-freaking-Beaufont. You do things the way you like, you challenge whenever you want, and you pass challenges by going to sleep instead of wearing yourself out for days. I suspect you'll be done with this one before the Castle is even rousing the others for breakfast."

"Oh. Well, thank you, sir," Sophia said, watching as Hiker muttered a series of incantations. She'd never seen him do magic quite like this, and it was thoroughly impressive. It was like a dancer doing ballet, captivating and original at the same time. She'd been around magicians all her life, and yet she'd never seen anyone do magic like Hiker Wallace.

A small boat that could only fit two people, or maybe one large one, or maybe one very large one and one tiny one, materialized in the water before them, sailing in their direction.

"Oh, bloody good. I call for a ship and I get a dinghy," Hiker complained, slapping his hands to his sides.

"We're sailing, sir?" she asked, remembering there was a sea creature that lived in the Pond who had tried to eat Wilder once when he went to retrieve the first bow ever made.

"Yes, but don't worry," Hiker said, pulling the boat onto the shore when it was close enough.

"Because you aren't going to rock the boat?" she asked.

"No, I will definitely do that," he said when she was in properly. He stepped in as he shoved off, looking out toward the coast on the other side. "But if you go overboard, I'll go too."

"Why is that, sir?" she asked.

"For one," he began, "if I return without you, Mama will have my ass."

"And the second part?" she dared to ask.

"If you tell anyone this, Sophia, I'll deny it vehemently," Hiker warned.

She nodded. "Go on, then."

"You, Sophia Beaufont, might be the person who saves us all."

She blinked at him in confusion. "Because I'm a woman and the Dragon Elite have never had one of those?"

He shook his head. "Because somehow, someway, you woke up the world. You woke me up, and here I am, sailing across the body of water that's been nestled outside my window for ages. I'm not thanking you, but I *am* blaming you. Thanks might come later."

Sophia smiled up at the leader of the Dragon Elite, enjoying sailing across the placid waters. "And cursed blame might also."

He nodded. "Yeah, it will be one or the other, but nothing in between."

Sophia held her chin up as they sailed to a part of the Gullington she'd never seen, enjoying the cold air and the excitement of a new challenge as the sun edged over the horizon.

CHAPTER THIRTY-THREE

When the small boat came to the opposite shore, it wasn't what Sophia had expected. She wasn't sure what she'd been expecting. Maybe a hotel and casino and some sort of challenge to her credibility or nobility or some other bility. What they came to was another shore like the one where they'd boarded the boat, but no castle rose out of the green hills, only a lot of rock structures and more hills.

Sophia jumped out of the boat and helped Hiker haul it onto the shore, to his obvious surprise. He arched an eyebrow at her. She gave him an expression of astonishment when he regarded her like she was a three-headed sheep.

"What?" she challenged. "What did I do *this* time?"

"I just expected you'd stay in the boat," he answered.

"And have you chariot me up to dry land?" she retorted. "You really have a thing or two to learn about modern women."

"Do they do everything for themselves these days?" he asked. "They don't expect us to throw our cloaks over a puddle, so they don't get their shoes wet?"

Sophia glanced back at Hiker. "Was that really a thing they did? That sounds awful. Why couldn't they just walk around?"

He actually laughed. "They could have. Ainsley used to, yelling at the other women that they were…" His voice trailed off, disappointing Sophia, who was wearing a curious expression.

"Anyway, I'm just surprised by you sometimes," Hiker remarked.

"And you, sir," Sophia said, her hands on her hips as she surveyed the green hills. "So what now? Where's the Starbucks?"

"The what?" he asked.

"The place where we get an overpriced coffee and a scone the size of our face," she answered.

He shook his head. "Scones should never be… Oh wait, that's one of those jokes you like to tell."

"It's a truthitude," Sophia told him. "But it's modern-world truth, so it's a joke wrapped in the real world, which is what makes it funny. Get it?"

He shook his head. "Like most of your jokes, no, not really."

"Well, this is going well," she said dryly, looking off across the Pond at the Castle in the distance.

"We are going to hike toward the caves," Hiker said, pointing up the hill.

"Cool," Sophia said, starting in that direction. "The ones up here? Or the ones towards the top?"

"Neither," Hiker answered. "The ones ten miles away."

Sophia halted, her face finally taking on an angry expression. "Ten miles? Really? And you threw away my supplies because allowing me water or refreshment was totally against the rules when the others had them?"

He shook his head at her, granting her no sympathy. "You're Sophia-freaking-Beaufont."

Hiker Wallace, without another word, ambled in the direction he'd indicated.

Sophia hurried to get in front of the large man. "What does that mean—'You're Sophia-freaking-Beaufont.' Is that an insult?"

Hiker regarded her for a long moment before shaking his

head. "Just the opposite. I just leveled the playing field. You're Sophia-freaking-Beaufont. Everything is easy for you. I send you to the Outback, and you don't fight. Now I'm going with you on the hardest part of the training. The hike isn't the worst part, but it's supposed to tire you out. Let's see how you do."

He edged around her and continued the trek.

Sophia didn't move. Instead, she put her hands on her hips and raised her chin. "Do you *want* me to fail, sir?"

He shook his head as he turned around to face her. "No, that's just the thing, Sophia. I've come to the point where I expect you to succeed, no matter the odds."

"I don't have it easy," she argued, sensing where he was going with this whole thing.

"I know," he replied almost on the heels of her words.

"I don't get all this given to me," she continued.

"I know that too."

"I've come by this through hard work," she insisted, unsure of what she was trying to prove.

"Sophia, do you know how many riders I've trained?"

She shook her head.

"More than you would expect. I've lost track at this point," Hiker answered. "They never make it this far in their training so fast with so many accolades. Many have died battling those zombie dogs in the Outback. I almost did. I didn't give you any provisions on this hike because you don't need them. I suspect we won't be out here long because I know what I have to do, and I think you'll figure it out faster than any of the others. Don't think this is favoritism, but you, Sophia freaking Beaufont, aren't like any other rider I've ever trained or known."

Sophia nearly choked after those words but recovered. "Thank you, sir."

"Don't thank me," he replied. "That might be a good thing or the death of us all. We will find out."

CHAPTER THIRTY-FOUR

In a perfect world, Sophia would have had a week or so to rest up after the Australian Outback before taking a ten-mile hike. However, she didn't live in a perfect world, even though she hoped to make it a better place. If she didn't kill Hiker on this arduous trek.

"So if you're hiking right now," Sophia began after they'd been silent for over an hour with only the sounds of their boots shuffling through the grass and the birds calling over the Pond. "Then it's Hiker hiking through the hikable hills, right?"

He sighed, obviously unimpressed by the little rhyme it had taken her over an hour to construct.

"We don't have to talk," he offered, stopping to rest at the top of a hill and pressing his hands into his lower back.

"What were you like as a child?" Sophia asked, unsure why she wanted to get under his skin so badly. It just seemed like the thing to do at this point. Yes, he'd been complimentary to her, but she thought it was him just being matter-of-fact. Hiker thought she was more than competent, but he also seemed really surprised by the idea like he was waiting for her to fail at some point and prove his initial judgment had been right all along.

"I was little," he answered, moving faster as they descended the hill.

"Were you playful or curious or mischievous?" she asked.

"We didn't play," he answered. "That was invented in the eighteenth century."

She nodded like this made perfect sense. "That explains it."

"And no, Thad was the mischievous one, as we've previously discussed," he went on.

"Right, and this is when you elaborate so we can have a meaningful conversation," Sophia suggested, still unsure why she was forcing conversation on Hiker. Something about these hills was encouraging her to talk, to want to learn, maybe even to tell her own story.

"I've always had rules," he began slowly, the words seeming difficult at first, like he was remembering something from long ago. "I crave order. Always have. If something is against the rules, I have a hard time even fathoming it. Thad, on the other hand, is exactly the opposite. He breaks the rules just for the fun of it. No respect for order or organization."

"So more like the 'ask for forgiveness rather than permission' type?" she inquired.

He shook his head. "I don't think he'd ever cared for forgiveness. And definitely not permission."

"Is it possible people are really born bad?" she mused, not wanting to believe such a notion. The far-reaching implications were too much. That meant prisons were necessary, and rehabilitation was less important. Sophia wanted to believe in a world where people were merely confused when they did wrong and could be taught to be better.

"I don't know," he said, considering the idea. "In Thad's case, I absolutely think so. I've met other dragonriders who were just like him, albeit not as evil. No one is quite like Thad in that regard."

"Other riders," Sophia contemplated. "Why do they seem so

black and white? Are they all either good or bad? Or are there a lot of gray ones too?"

"Not that I'm aware of," Hiker said. "Most I've encountered fall on one end of the spectrum or the other. There isn't much in between."

"That's weird," Sophia stated. "I grew up with many different magician families, and they were all over the place. Most were good, being associated with the House of Fourteen, but there was always some bad to the people. Even I have been known to steal a donut from the kitchen on occasion."

"Get out!" Hiker yelled, turning abruptly to face Sophia, his face serious.

She halted, looking at him with mild annoyance. "Oh, shush it." Sophia hiked around him and took the lead.

"What were *you* like as a child?" Hiker asked after a moment.

She glanced at him, surprised by the question. "Little," Sophia answered, sticking her tongue out at him.

He rolled his eyes. "I mean, I get it's the sort of question that answers itself since you're still a child in many regards."

"I'm eighteen," she fired back.

"You're a child until you celebrate your hundredth birthday in my eyes."

"Is that when I get my cookie bouquet?" she asked.

He shook his head. "You get one on your five-hundredth birthday, just like I did."

"What did you do for your five-hundredth birthday?" she asked.

"You first," he insisted. "I asked you a question, and you haven't answered it. What were you like as a child? More of a child than you are now."

She thought for a moment, trying to figure out how to describe herself. "I was lonely."

The expression that crossed his face made her rush into an explanation.

"I'm not saying that for sympathy," she explained. "That's a fact. My older siblings had full-time responsibilities as Warrior and Councilor for the House of Fourteen, as well as taking care of our parent's business. Clark was always studying. Liv...well, she left before I can remember. For years, it was just me and my magic. No one could know I had it, though; Reese and Ian were clear on that point. So most of my education was private tutoring or just on my own. I didn't really want to play with the other kids anyway because they always found me strange, although I don't know why."

"Because you were born as an authority," Hiker said matter-of-factly.

"What?" she asked.

"All dragonriders are, according to *The Complete History of Dragonriders*. You remember, my book that you lost," he teased with a serious expression on his face.

"I didn't lose it," she protested. "Trinity took it and is keeping it in the Great Library."

"Which we currently have a portal open to in the Castle, thanks to you."

"You're welcome," she chirped.

"Anyway, I haven't read all of the book, and I don't remember a great deal of it," Hiker continued. "What I do recall states that dragonriders, since they are intended to be adjudicators, are born with a natural authority. When you were young, if you told a playmate to do something, did they?"

Sophia thought for a moment, trailing back in her mind to a distant memory. "Yeah, I guess they did. I always thought that was because I'm bossy."

"You are that," Hiker said. "But it's a bit more than just because you're a rider. We have a natural capacity as judges. Our rule strikes an accord in many."

"But this doesn't work on other riders, does it?" Sophia asked. "That's why you could never make Thad behave?"

Hiker nodded. "It's the ironic part of all of this. We bring order and justice, and our history has shown those we fight most often are ourselves. Other riders have usually been the instigators—the ones who threatened the peace we worked so hard for."

"Wow," Sophia mused. "Maybe it would be better if there were no more dragonriders."

Again, Hiker halted and faced her. "Don't say something like that."

"But sir," Sophia began, "we serve an important role, but if most of our efforts are in trying to make other riders behave, maybe it's just better if there aren't riders."

Hiker swallowed, a sober expression in his eyes. "I get your logic, but I have to believe the good riders bring more peace than the bad ones bring evil. And besides, there is only one bad dragonrider left. Once Thad is gone, then we can reign."

"Have you considered how you're going to take him down?" Sophia dared to ask.

A small stress line formed around Hiker's jaw. "I believe that's why I'm on this trek with you. So no, but hopefully on the way back, the answer will be different."

"Do we have to hike back, or can we grab an Uber?" Sophia joked.

"A what?" Hiker asked.

She waved him off. "It was one of those jokes you love so much and rarely get."

The pair hiked on for another hour in silence. Sophia was good with it, grateful they had a bit of conversation.

When they came to a cave opening surrounded by rectangular columns, Hiker paused.

"That's far out," Sophia said, admiring the stone structures which lined the sides of the cave. The blocks were so orderly they appeared man made, although it seemed unlikely.

"There's another more well-known cave on the other side of

Scotland like this called Fingal's Cave," Hiker explained. "Mortals know about that one, but not Falconer Cave."

"Falconer?" Sophia asked. "Like the people who tame birds and wear eye patches?"

"I wasn't aware of the eye patch part, but yes," he answered.

"Well, I don't think they start off with it," Sophia joked. "Maybe just the really bad ones get their eyes poked out by the bird of prey."

"You're very strange," he observed.

"So, what's with this cave?" Sophia asked, studying the strange hexagonal columns which marked the entrance. "Does it have strange magical significance?"

Hiker shook his head. "The acoustics are good."

Sophia rolled her eyes. "Did you bring me out here to sing?"

"There will definitely not be any singing," Hiker answered. "The cave's acoustics are important for this part of the training."

"Because?" Sophia asked.

"You'll find out." Hiker strode onward a few paces before turning back to Sophia. "For my five-hundredth birthday, I had a glass of whisky and a quiet evening to myself."

"So it was pretty much like every day before," Sophia stated.

He nodded. "When you get to be as old as I am, the birthdays roll together."

"Well, maybe for your next birthday, someone will throw you a party with streamers and cake."

He scowled at her. "That person wouldn't see another of *their* birthdays."

Sophia laughed. "You and your threats are so cute."

CHAPTER THIRTY-FIVE

"Why didn't you tell me I needed to dress up?" Sophia joked when they entered Falconer Cave.

"Ha-ha," Hiker said with no humor, his voice echoing. The cavernous space was dark and cold, like most caves. However, there was something unique about the stillness in here, but Sophia couldn't put her finger on what it was.

"What are we supposed to do?" Sophia asked, looking around as her eyes adjusted to the dark.

"Sit and be quiet," he answered.

"You made me hike ten miles to a cave with fantastic acoustics so I could sit and be quiet?" she challenged. "You get why this might be the site of a murder, right?"

"First of all, I was your gillie, making your task of finding Falconer Cave easier," Hiker stated.

"'Gillie?'" she questioned. "Are you making up words again?"

He shook his head. "'Gillie' is a Scottish term for a guide who attends men while exploring the Highlands or hunting or fishing. They know the land better than anyone."

Sophia cleared her throat and gave him a pointed look.

Hiker rolled his eyes. "Sophia, I can't change history. In the past, gillies accompanied men. Women didn't hunt, so that's the reason for the definition I gave you."

"Okay, fine," she acquiesced. "You were my gillie and helped me find Falconer Cave."

He nodded. "It took Evan a week because usually I just point to the general vicinity and tell people what to look for."

Sophia recalled the unique outward appearance of the cave. "Yeah, it would be easy to spot."

"Second of all," he continued, "the point of this training exercise is to get quiet."

"Which is why you do it in a place with great acoustics?" Sophia questioned.

"The acoustics help by magnifying the quiet," Hiker explained.

"Isn't that like multiplying something by zero?"

He simply shook his head before settling down on the rocky ground and crossing his legs.

"Oh, you are serious about this being quiet business, aren't you?"

"It is through meditation we come to understand ourselves, receive insights on problems, and become one with the universe," Hiker explained in a rehearsed manner.

Sophia settled on the ground. "Mama Jamba sent you out here because you've got to face Thad and don't know how?"

"Correct," he agreed. "I've never known how, but we always have an opportunity to become better than we were. To figure out the things that eluded us. But we have to do the work for it. Usually, that involves going within and finding our connection to the universe. It is there the answers are born."

"So, it's kind of like the whole idea that we're not in the universe, the universe is within us," Sophia stated.

He nodded, his hands casually resting on his knees, back straight and face calm. "Your experience meditating will be unique to you and what you need to know. I will offer this bit of advice: to connect with yourself, you must first connect with the world around you. Falconer Cave is ideal because it is isolated from everything around it, it is an anomaly unique on the outside and bare on the inside."

"Okay," Sophia said, drawing out the word. "When do I know I've achieved the training goal?"

"You will know," he said simply.

"Will you stop inundating me with information," she joked.

Hiker closed his eyes. "Do you hear that?"

Sophia paused. Listened. "What? I don't hear anything."

"Exactly," he said. "When you hear the voices of the angels and all their messages, that's when you're done. When you no longer have questions and intuitively know answers to things yet to be asked, you're done. When you can hear the spirit of the universe within you, you can go."

CHAPTER THIRTY-SIX

Sophia didn't think she could simply pretend she'd heard the voices of the angels and pop out of the cave early. She'd meditated a time or two, but she'd never gotten much out of it besides a nap.

This was the strangest training exercise. How was she supposed to connect with herself or the universe? And how would she know when she'd achieved it? Would the messages from the angels sound different from the ramblings in her head?

Hiker seemed to think Sophia would have an easy time with this, which was why he had thrown her supplies out. After the long hike, she wished she had some water. Or a protein bar. Or a bed.

Her mind began to wander, combing over what she needed to do later. Then it drifted to all the chaos going on all over the world as a result of Thad Reinhart's planning. She hadn't been on any adjudicator missions in a while. That worried her. But she'd been busy with training and before that finding *The Complete History of Dragonriders*.

There was nothing like seeing the gold dust over an agreement struck between two parties who were once opposed, she thought, her mind quickly jumping around. After a long while of this, Sophia realized how loud her thoughts were, as if the cave was amplifying them. They were inundating and seemingly unending, one thought leading to another and then another.

Taking a breath, she tried to stop her thoughts, which were like a contagious disease, spreading fast. It seemed strange to stop thinking. That seemed as easy as stopping breathing.

It was breathing that helped the most. When she focused on her breath, the thoughts slowed down and became less intense. After a bit, Sophia noticed her breath had elongated and her thoughts had followed suit, passing through her brain slowly and then drifting away. Whereas before she had judged every thought as good or bad, soon she found she was simply an observer, taking notice of the ideas without coloring them one way or another.

Soon her focus shifted to the area around her in the cave. She felt outside of herself in a very distinctive way. The temperature, she knew without knowing how, was exactly fifty degrees. There were sixteen different species that called Falconer Cave home. Of those, three were magical and unclassified, one of which was presently crawling on Sophia's boot.

She didn't feel the little creature but instinctively knew it was there. Usually, she would have jumped up and brushed the bug off. However, Sophia didn't even think of it as something else on her. She was the bug, and the bug was her. They were the cave, and the cave was them. They were the Gullington, and the Gullington was them. They were Scotland, and Scotland was them. They were the universe, and the universe was them.

These observations were followed by a strange silence that seemed to stretch on for eternity. It was this silence that had preceded Mother Nature and spawned a creature so powerful she could construct a world that was strong and also vulnerable. It was this silence that had filled the void before time was created. Before Papa Creola constructed how events moved on a continuum. The silence was the beginning, and it was every-where still.

Sophia didn't know how long she sat in the cave, witnessing the birth of the universe in her mind. It could have been a minute or a hundred years. If it had been more than a day, she didn't feel hungry or tired or thirsty. She had hooked into the nourishment of the universe, and she realized as long as she was connected, all her needs were fulfilled.

From that place, Sophia knew she could heal the world's problem. She could erase the pain. She could become whatever she wanted. The idea of never leaving Falconer Cave was very tempting. She could fix everything just by maintaining her connection to the all-powerful source.

There were things she'd miss. Her friends growing old. Her family loving her. The opportunity to see tragedy and heroically risk everything for justice.

Yes, there were problems in the world she could mend in Falconer Cave with her mind, but it didn't mean she should. Being out in the world as a player on the chessboard was more important. Interacting with other players was part of a valuable experience for Sophia and for them.

Being a part of the world is more important than fixing it, she real-ized. *A perfect world was never the point.*

Sophia's eyes sprang open, and she knew instinctively she'd arrived where she needed to be. Her training in Falconer Cave was done. The angels had spoken to her, and they'd said, "You in an imperfect world is better than a perfect world without you. Wake up, our love. Go out and spawn a new age, Sophia Beaufont the Great."

CHAPTER THIRTY-SEVEN

Hiker wasn't in Falconer Cave when Sophia opened her eyes. The sun was streaming through the opening when she rose, but she didn't know how much time had passed. It could have been years for all she knew.

Upon exiting the cave, she found Hiker leaning against the outside wall with his foot up behind him. Bell and Lunis were in the distance, resting in the grass.

He eyed his watch when he saw her and nodded. "As I suspected. That's a new record."

"How long was I in there?" Sophia asked. "Did I exceed Evan's twelve weeks, or however long it took him to phone the angels?"

He shook his head. "No, you just made the record for the shortest amount of time."

"What?" she asked, surprised.

"It took you just a wee bit over an hour," Hiker explained, glancing at the Expanse where the dragons lay. Lunis was gesturing in playful ways, and Bell was doing her best to ignore him.

"Why do you think that is?" Sophia asked, sincerely wanting

an answer to why she excelled. It all felt like a trick. Like false confidence she didn't want to fall for.

"I think a lot of it has to do with the fact you're a twin and he's dead," Hiker began. "I know that doesn't make you feel better because losing a twin, even if you didn't know him, is still tragic in its own way. The angels say twins are forever connected and share a unique power. But his death did grant you benefits to your magic."

Sophia nodded. She didn't mind that as an explanation so much. It wasn't something she controlled, though. In a way, she'd prefer to be as successful as she was because she worked hard for it and not because she inherited Jamison's power.

"But also," Hiker continued. "I think your gender grants you a unique perspective. As dragonriders and men, we do things a certain way. We always have. We rush into battle. Our instinct is to fight. Often the chi of the dragon takes us over, bringing out our aggression and ruling over us if we're not careful. But women are quite different. Your nature is to nurture, to create, to mend and gather. I think that's why you consider solutions to your problems that never occur to us."

Sophia nodded again, chewing her lip. Once more, this made sense, but it also attributed her success to a factor she didn't control. Her success being tied to her gender didn't make her feel any better.

"Then there's the fact that you're the first female dragonrider," Hiker went on. "I mistakenly believed you were elected to this position because you inherited your twin's power early, making you an exceptional magician. However, the angels have shown me something different."

"In your meditation just now?" she asked.

He nodded. "You're not the first magician to have their twin die at birth and receive their powers from the beginning. There are many records of this since it's a point of interest. The incredible, from an early age, have notoriously done one thing."

He paused, almost like he was begging her to urge him to continue.

After a moment, Hiker cleared his throat. "There's a reason children don't have magic. There's a reason education usually precedes the onset of magical abilities after the start of puberty. Magic held by children turns into instant gratification. In essence, it corrupts." He shook his head. "But we always have a choice, even as children. It's like when the universe presents different signs to you. Many think the signs are directing their path, but they're wrong. It's the ones you endorse, the ones you want to come true, that creates the path. You might be powerful because of something you don't control. You might be unique as a dragonrider because of your gender. But you're inevitably successful because of who you are and the choices you make. Sophia, you are good through and through, and the only one the angels have met who wasn't ruined by magic given at an early age."

Sophia blinked at him, utterly confused. "Your meditation was about me?"

He pursed his lips, seeming to share her confusion. "Yes, I was seeking solutions to how to deal with my own twin, and I received information about you. Who knows why, but I can't question the methods of the angels. They are never wrong."

"Okay," she said, continuing to chew her lip as she tried to absorb everything Hiker had shared. Sophia remembered being young and knowing she could have anything she wanted because of her magic—and she remembered knowing that if something didn't belong to her or it was wrong, it wasn't worth having. From the beginning, Sophia hadn't refrained from doing things out of fear of punishment. She'd refrained because being good felt good, and feeling good was what it was about for everyone at the end of the day.

"Oh, and Sophia?" Hiker resumed, pulling her out of her thoughts.

"Yes, sir?" she answered.

"The angels also told me you're exceptional because you are the first female rider," Hiker explained. "Just as Alexander Conerly, the very first dragonrider, was exceptional. That's how the angels intended it because we are the adjudicators for this world. We serve Mother Nature. We are supposed to be a force. The first of something must always be great, so others follow them. They make history and a name for themselves and that which they represent. So there you go—you're successful because you're a twin, you're a female, and you're the first. But also, and most importantly, remember you are successful because of what you choose."

He sighed and looked at the dragons. "My only regret at this point is the age of the dragons and their riders are dying. I would have liked to have seen a world with more female dragonriders. Maybe a year ago, I wouldn't have, but you've changed that. I think you provide a balance we desperately need, but alas, we are nearing our end."

Sophia found it hard to swallow. "Don't give up, sir. We never know how the universe will provide solutions." She glanced back at Falconer Cave, warmth spreading through her abdomen. "And although the angels didn't tell you how to defeat Thad, maybe they gave you a new motivation to do so."

CHAPTER THIRTY-EIGHT

W hen they returned to the Castle, Mama Jamba was curled up on the couch in Hiker's office, watching the movie *Beaches*, tears flowing down her face.

"Mama, why are you torturing yourself like this?" Hiker asked, shaking his head as he stomped into his study.

She sniffed. "Because if I'm going to be sad, then at least I'll be entertained. I could watch the news you have broadcasting and be sad about what's happening to my planet, but that's not what I want to do."

Hiker picked up the top newspaper from the stack on his desk that had just been delivered to his office via Ainsley. He shook his head. "It's getting worse. Countries are battling, threatening one another with deadly force and weapons of mass destruction."

"Oh, and the Golden Globes are coming up according to one of the articles in the *LA Times*," Ainsley said as she cleaned up all the used tissues scattered around Mama Jamba. She looked up at Sophia. "What are the Golden Globes?"

Sophia waved her off. "Nothing of interest."

Ainsley nodded dutifully and continued to pick up.

"How is it that one man could cause such global discord?" Sophia asked.

Hiker shook his head. "Thad has a lot of power and skill. If he ever committed to using it for good, he could have done great things. But that was never his way."

"Hiker, you look a hundred years younger," Ainsley observed. "Have you been using that face cream in S. Beaufont's room too?"

Sophia glanced abruptly at the housekeeper. "Is that where my lotion keeps going?"

The shapeshifter nodded, no guilt on her face. "Oh, yes. Quiet likes it too. Although he uses it mostly on his feet."

Sophia grimaced, hoping the gnome washed his hands before dipping into her lotion. "Is there no privacy in this place?"

"Of course, there is," Ainsley commented. "Oh, and by the way, you've been talking in your sleep a lot S. Apparently, you have a crush on a Scotsman, but I can't figure out any more than that. Can you talk a bit clearer in the future?"

Sophia's eyes fluttered with annoyance. "I do not have a crush. I have a bunch of dirty Scotsmen around me who burp at the dining table and chew with their mouths open, which is why they invade my dreams. My subconscious is obviously trying to work through the frustration the only way it knows how. And would you kindly not watch me when I sleep?"

Ainsley held up her hands as if in surrender. "Don't watch you when you sleep. Don't drug your food. Stop using your clothes to dust the rafters. You always have so many rules, S. Beaufont. But fine, I'll try and mind your privacy. No promises, though."

Mama Jamba wailed as she focused on the television. "Oh, Bette Midler is just brilliant in this movie. What is she doing these days, I wonder?"

"Mama, don't you think there's anything else you could direct your attention to?" Hiker asked, irritation in his tone. "You do remember war is brewing all over your planet, right?"

The old woman looked up briefly, seemingly stuck in a daze. "That's a great idea. I should pay Papa Creola a visit."

"Do you think he can help us?" Hiker asked, hope in his voice.

She shrugged. "Who knows, but I'm thinking of asking him to extend Bette's timeline. That way, she has more time to do great things."

Hiker threw the newspaper on his desk. "Am I the only sane one here?"

"If you are, then we're all in trouble because you lost your marbles a long time ago," Ainsley said. "And again, why do you look good enough to snog?"

Hiker gave her a repulsed expression. "Would you mind your tongue?"

She giggled. "Not by me. Maybe by Bell or Quiet. Or Evan. He's been wanting to lay a sloppy one on you for ages. I've heard him say it in his sleep."

"Evan is simply trying to suck up to authority," Mama Jamba supplied. "He will outgrow it in a few hundred years. Hiker is looking refreshed because I sent him to Falconer Cave."

"Oh, a good meditation is really great for the complexion," Ainsley said, looking at Sophia. "You went too? You look simply radiant. But you all weren't gone for a fortnight."

"No, Sophia is a quick study," Mama Jamba offered. "And Hiker knew what he was looking for, so his job should have been quick. Tell me, son, where is Thad, and how are you planning on taking him down?"

Hiker shook his head. "I don't know. The angels didn't tell me. Why don't you tell me?"

Mama Jamba returned her attention to the television. "You know I can't do that, Hiker. You have to fight your battles on your own. Tough love, you get it."

"You want me to protect your Earth. Save it. But you're unwilling to offer me anything?" he asked.

She nodded. "That's right, dear. I trust you'll get it done with the resources at your disposal...or you won't, and we'll all die from some nuclear explosions." She shrugged. "Can't wait to find out how this story ends."

"Resources," Hiker muttered, looking around his office. "I've got a globe that doesn't work on my brother, a bunch of newspapers that tell me war is imminent, television screens with anxious reporters who offer more opinion than fact, and not much else."

"Actually, sir, I might have a way of helping us to find Thad," Sophia offered.

Mama Jamba pulled a Twizzler from a package she hadn't had a few seconds earlier and took a bite. She pointed at Sophia. "Resources, Hiker. They are everywhere. They are people. Remember that."

He turned his attention to Sophia. "What do you mean?"

"Well, since I know Thad uses magitech heavily," Sophia began, "I took the gun Logan used on Lunis and me to my scientist friend. She's our foremost expert on magitech. Anyway, she's been working on a way to track the epicenter of where the magitech is originating. The source, if you will. She says hiding that kind of power is difficult. I can check with her and find out where she is with the process."

"You did this without my permission, going off on your own and taking initiative?" Hiker asked with a threat in his voice.

Sophia bowed her head, sighing. "I'm sorry, sir. I just thought—"

"No apologies," he interrupted. "Good work. And yes, you should check in with her."

"She also thinks she might be able to find other ways to fight Thad, circumventing security measures and whatnot," Sophia said, feeling proud.

"You mean, technology?" Hiker asked.

"You will have to embrace it if you're going to fight him," Mama Jamba said, chewing on the end of a red Twizzler.

"You have already allowed televisions into the Castle," Ainsley pointed out.

"That's different," he argued. "I need information and fast, and that seemed like the best way."

Ainsley smirked at him. "It's only a matter of time before you're sporting a phone and dragging around a shiny lapbottom."

"Laptop," Sophia corrected.

Hiker let out a weighty breath. "Yeah, I don't think so. This is ultimately my fight with my brother, and I'll do it the way I see fit. I don't believe it will involve technology. However, getting to Thad might involve magitech, I'll give you that much."

"You think by taking down Thad, you'll stop all the wars that are brewing?" Ainsley asked, reading one of the newspapers upside-down. "Don't you think the wars he's started will just continue? He's set the balls in motion."

For a brief moment, Sophia saw a shimmer of the person Ainsley used to be. She had been a diplomat for the elves, offering strategic advice to the Dragon Elite. It shone through for a moment, making the usually silly housekeeper appear refined and serious. Sophia wasn't sure which version of Ainsley she preferred. Maybe a mix of both.

"But he's the kindling, dear," Mama Jamba explained. "Take out that which causes the fire, and the adjudicators can do what they do best. I fear if they tried to intervene now, it would be a losing battle. Hate fuels hate. It has to be erased, and then love can grow."

Hiker nodded and gave the old woman a proud smile. "That's the helpful advice I've been looking for."

"Oh, before I forget," Ainsley said, looking at Hiker, "you got a message from the House of Fourteen saying they are freaking out about this war business and ready to take over, since, and I quote, 'the Dragon Elite can't do their job.'"

He lowered his chin and regarded her with hooded eyes. "When did this message come in?"

"A few days ago," she replied.

"Why are you just telling me now?" he questioned.

"Because you were all holed up in your office, fretting that something had happened to S. Beaufont in the Australian Outback," she answered. "I didn't want to add more stress."

"I wasn't fretting," he argued, cutting his eyes to Sophia briefly. "As your leader, it is my job to be concerned about your wellbeing and focused on your success."

"Right," Ainsley chirped. "That's why he kept pacing in his office and overworking his hair while he muttered, 'Stay vigilant, Soph. Fight the dogs. Come back in one piece.'"

Hiker gave Sophia a sympathetic look. "I echo what you said about us having more privacy in this place."

CHAPTER THIRTY-NINE

The portal Sophia had opened up between the Castle and House of Fourteen might have irritated Hiker, but it made her commute a lot easier.

She found the closet door exactly where it had been in the corridor outside her room. She didn't need the gold token to go back and forth anymore, but she always kept it on her since she was the new keeper of the reset point.

Holding the coin in her hand, Sophia considered Hiker's last request before she'd exited his office moments prior.

"Meet with this scientist friend of yours," he had requested with authority. "Hopefully, she can help us find Thad. But before that, go tell the House of Fourteen they don't need to intervene in this matter. We are in charge of world affairs. We are the adjudicators for this planet. The Dragon Elite has this."

Sophia had been impressed by the leader of the Dragon Elite's confidence. It had changed since Falconer Cave. Hiker appeared more like the person he had been when she saw him during the reset point at the House of Fourteen.

Then he had urged the council to take action, explaining a war was brewing, and they'd dismissed him. This made her worry that her statement to the House of Fourteen would be ignored too. If they didn't take the leader of the Dragon Elite seriously, would they accept her word? A lot had changed since then, and the council was made up of new members. She hoped they'd be reasonable.

Sophia stepped into the closet like she had done before and closed the door. She was instantly cloaked in blackness. After a quick three count, Sophia opened the door to find the rush of old smells and sights greeting her eyes.

The House of Fourteen's dark wooden walls and intricate crown molding was such a contrast to the Castle with its cold stone and high ceilings. Similar to the Castle, the walls of the House were decorated with paintings of its members, and there were various artifacts on display in different areas.

Ignoring all this, Sophia made her way straight to the Chamber of the Tree, wanting to catch the Council before they were dismissed.

She was surprised to find her brother Clark pacing outside the entrance to the Chamber in front of the Door of Reflection.

He glanced up as she approached, relief on his face. "There you are. You're late."

She halted, confused. "I didn't realize we had a planned meeting."

"Well, we didn't," he explained, leaning forward and whispering, "Hester told me Trudy saw a vision of you visiting the House of Fourteen today and that it would be my best opportunity to catch you. I figured you were coming to explain why the Dragon Elite are failing in their mission."

Sophia let out a frustrated breath. "I have no intention of explaining anything to the council." She'd been struggling to find the right thing to say to the House of Fourteen based on what Hiker had said, but now, she knew exactly how to play things.

"Regardless," Clark continued in a hushed voice, "I suspect

Bianca and Lorenzo are going to suggest a Dragon Elite take a place on the council."

Sophia nodded. She remembered overhearing their conversation when she was hiding in the Mantovanis' residence. "Yes, they think if they give us enough rope, we'll hang ourselves, mortals will hate us, and tension will break out on the council."

"Exactly," he affirmed. "That's why when they offer you a position, which I firmly believe they will, you should decline."

"Why?" Sophia questioned. "Do you think we will screw things up and cause a revolt?"

Uncertainty crossed Clark's face as he hesitated to answer.

"Are you serious?" Sophia nearly yelled. "You doubt us?"

He sighed. "It's not that, Soph. Of course, I believe in *you*, but the Dragon Elite aren't giving us much confidence. From our perspective, Hiker Wallace has been sticking his head in the sand, allowing Thad Reinhart to become more powerful."

"It's all by design," she fibbed.

Clark pursed his lips. "But really, I think you should decline the position because then you can't be held accountable."

"I will decline the position, but not for that reason," Sophia stated.

"What is the reason?" he asked.

She couldn't help but be angry at her brother, although she knew he was just looking at things the way he always did—logically. Sophia couldn't totally disagree with his perspective or the opinion the House of Fourteen had of the current situation. Hiker had made mistakes, but that put him in a perfect position to make better choices. She firmly believed he was the only one who could end Thad Reinhart.

What scared her, when she allowed herself to admit it, was that Thad was probably the only one who could end Hiker. If that happened, she feared the Dragon Elite were done for good.

If something happened to Hiker, it would be the end of an era.

CHAPTER FORTY

The Chamber of the Tree was buzzing when Sophia stepped through the Door of Reflection a few minutes after Clark, so as to not make it obvious they had been talking.

Jude, the white tiger, stood on one side of the bench, his discerning eyes watching Sophia. Conversely, Diabolos, the black crow, took flight at the sight of her and perched close to the ceiling, which shimmered with twinkling lights.

Many of the Warriors were absent from the proceedings, off on missions. Thankfully, Liv wasn't. It gave Sophia confidence to know her sister was there standing stoically at her back.

She strode straight into the round room, taking the position in the center between the arc of Warriors and Councilors.

"Sophia Beaufont," Haro Takahashi began when she paused. "Have you come to update us on how the Dragon Elite is going to deal with Thad Reinhart?"

Shaking her head, Sophia put her hands behind her back. "No, I have not."

"You haven't?" Lorenzo Rosario asked, stroking his black goatee. "Then why are you here?"

"To tell you the situation is under control," Sophia answered.

Bianca Mantovani laughed, a cold, high-pitched sound. "Oh, that's too much. Even to those who don't follow world affairs, it's obvious you all don't have anything under control. Mayhem is breaking out everywhere, perpetuated by—"

"We are fully aware of the global events," Sophia interrupted.

"Then how does the Dragon Elite plan to deal with the situation that's building?" Lorenzo asked.

"We do not answer to the Council for the House of Fourteen," Sophia declared. "We supersede your authority, and therefore, I'm not at liberty to say."

"With all due respect," Lorenzo countered, his tone dripping with condescension, "we haven't seen anything like this since—"

"Right before the Great War broke out, which made it so mortals couldn't see magic and our history was forgotten," Sophia cut in. "Hiker warned you it would happen, and the Council ignored him. With all due respect, the Dragon Elite aren't in a position where we feel the need to explain our plans to you. We are back. We are prepared to handle Thad Reinhart. We plan to restore our reputation and status as world adjudicators. That is all you need to know."

Lorenzo lowered his chin, giving her a petulant expression, suddenly making Sophia feel small. She reminded herself she wasn't. She was a dragonrider and not the littlest Beaufont, as many from the House of Fourteen were used to seeing her. "Why can't Hiker Wallace report to us himself?"

"That's a good question," Bianca agreed, looking down the bench at Lorenzo. "If the leader of the Dragon Elite wants us to have confidence in his ability to handle this situation, he should at least meet with us, especially after we sent a message to him directly."

"He is just a tad bit busy," Liv said at Sophia's back.

"Warrior Beaufont," Lorenzo scolded, "I don't believe this matter involves you."

"Yes, just because your little sister is here, it doesn't mean you have to step in and save her," Bianca added snootily.

"No one needs to save me," Sophia said boldly. "I'm a rider for the Dragon Elite, and I'm here by order of Hiker Wallace, who is concerned with more pressing matters. He asked me to pass along to you, the House of Fourteen, that there is no need for you to intervene in the Thad Reinhart situation. It is under control, and we need no help."

"I am sure you are correct," Hester DeVries began in a calm voice. "However, pooling our resources might be for the best. The Dragon Elite's numbers aren't what they once were and fighting such a formidable force; well, it could destroy you all. We can offer assistance." She held out her hand, indicating Liv and the others standing at Sophia's back. "How about the help of our Warriors?"

"That won't be necessary," Sophia said at once. "Thank you for the offer, but as world adjudicators, we prefer to handle this situation on our own."

"This is ridiculous!" Lorenzo exclaimed. "You are going to start a war we can't control or extinguish."

"No," Sophia fired. "We are going to prevent a war."

"What if," Bianca began slowly, looking between the various council members, "I know we haven't discussed this, but what if we invited the Dragon Elite to have a place on the council? It's just an idea, but maybe then they would be more willing to share their plans and have our input."

There was a collective murmur from the Councilors.

"We would decline such an invitation," Sophia interrupted, making all of them go silent.

"But you haven't even brought the request to your leader," Lorenzo argued.

"I don't need to," Sophia said with conviction. "The Dragon Elite does not work for the House of Fourteen. We do not need a place on the council. Although our numbers are small, it is important you recognize the hierarchy that was set up long ago. The Dragon Elite might have been gone for a long time, but we are back now, and we rank above the House of Fourteen and every other magical organization."

"With all due respect—" Lorenzo began once again.

Sophia rolled her eyes. "Would you stop saying that phrase since you absolutely intend disrespect by arguing with me?"

Lorenzo's mouth hung open for a moment, his eyes wide.

"Now," Sophia continued, "the Dragon Elite will deal with Thad Reinhart. We will reinstate order and take back our roles as adjudicators. This situation brewing worldwide is crucial to reset the stage."

This caused a great deal of chatter around the room. Sophia paused. She had just been making things up, but this sounded perfect. Hiker had allowed Thad to start these global events because how better to debut in this century as adjudicators? It hadn't been planned, but it made sense.

The Dragon Elite could have intervened in tons of small events to earn back their title, but it wouldn't have been as impactful. When they settled this dispute by putting out the fires of impending wars and taking Thad down, there would be no question they were the supreme authority.

All governments worldwide would endorse them as world adjudicators once more.

Haro Takahashi leaned forward. "I hope what you say is correct, Sophia. The world needs the Dragon Elite back in power."

"I understand you declining the position on the council," Raina Ludwig said, glancing down the bench at Bianca. "After further thought, that's like us inviting Father Time to have a vote when his authority surpasses ours. I apologize for any offense the offer caused."

Sophia nodded, surprised at how she'd played things. She always thought having a seat on the council as a dragonrider would be in everyone's best interest. If the Dragon Elite were going to come back into power, they had to claim their position, ranking above all.

CHAPTER FORTY-ONE

"That was freaking awesome!" Liv exclaimed as they walked to John's electronics repair shop. "You socked those jerks who were trying to get all up in your business."

Sophia blushed, pushing her hair behind her ears. "Clark doubts we have the Thad situation under control."

Liv rolled her eyes. "Good. Let him underestimate you. Let the council. That's for the best. That way, when you crush things, they will be that much more impressed. I usually like to put myself at a serious disadvantage before I claim the decisive victory no one saw coming. It's way more satisfying to see everyone's face then."

"The council has good reason to doubt us," Sophia confessed. "I mean, I respect Hiker, but I don't know if he can stand up to his brother when the time comes."

"Well, you didn't let them see that concern, which is crucial," Liv declared.

"Yeah, it was sort of a 'fake it until you feel it' thing," Sophia admitted.

Liv shook her head. "No, not at all. You were right to decline a position on the council. That would have made the dragonriders their equal, and you're not. You were also correct not to divulge your plans for Thad Reinhart. It's not their business. We preside over magical affairs and the Dragon Elite over mortal ones. The council has to find their place, and you did a good job of putting them there."

Sophia's nose twitched. "Well, honestly, between you and me, I couldn't have told them about our plans to deal with Thad since we don't have any. I'm hoping Alicia can help me. Otherwise, we might be screwed."

Liv offered her an encouraging expression. "If anyone can help you locate that magitech-wielding madman, it's Alicia. She's been working on it nonstop, which is why your 3D printer still isn't ready."

Sophia laughed. "I'm okay with that, and happy to have the help." Remembering the gift from Wilder, she smiled. "Oh, guess what I got for Christmas?"

"What?" Liv asked.

Liv clapped her hands to her chest when Sophia told her. "A man after my own heart. If he had given you chocolate or a gift card, I would have said to kick him to the curb, but a grappling hook? He's a keeper."

Sophia shook her head. "It's not like that. It was just a gift, and probably only because I was the one who pushed for Christmas to happen at the Castle. I gave him a fork."

With a laugh, Liv said, "Oh, that's perfect. Are you going to teach him how to use it?"

"Get out of my head," Sophia replied. "That's what I promised him. In return, he's supposed to teach me how to use the grappling hook."

Liv waved her off. "Oh, you don't need training. It's like this: you point and shoot, then get hauled off your butt. You're going to love it."

Sophia gave her an affectionate smile. "You think there was

ever a potential for us to have normal jobs and not ones where grappling hooks were a part of our routine?"

"Not a chance," Liv said, striding into the electronics shop.

Pickles, the Jack Russell terrier, greeted them by barking while he danced around their feet in excitement.

Sophia leaned down and gave the dog a quick pet before smiling at Alicia, who was working at a nearby station.

"Good timing," the scientist said, screwing something into the back of a small silver disc. "I was just finishing up the tracking device."

"Oh!" Sophia exclaimed. "You were able to create something?"

Alicia turned the small object over. It resembled a compass, although there were a lot more symbols on it other than just north, south, east, and west. "I think so, although it still needs to be calibrated. And…" Her face fell with concern.

"What?" Sophia asked, sensing the hesitation.

"Well, this device can find great sources of magitech," Alicia explained. "Which will lead you to possible locations for this Thad Reinhart."

"But it could also lead us in the wrong direction," Sophia guessed.

The scientist nodded. "What you'd need to ensure it sends you in the right direction is some sort of connection to the person you're trying to find. That way magitech takes a two-pronged approached. It first searches for high levels of magitech energy, then narrows them down based on DNA. I realize you probably don't have some hair samples of Thad lying around."

"Actually, what about blood from a really close relative?" Sophia asked.

Alicia's face brightened. "That could work, but how close? Like, distant cousin would get you close, but probably not enough."

"Would twin brother work?" Sophia asked.

Alicia slipped the compass-like device into a small velvet

pouch and handed it to Sophia. "Yes, that's perfect, actually. Have this twin brother follow the instructions I've included in the pouch to connect the device to Thad. If done correctly, it will take up to two days to activate."

"I hope you have that kind of time," Liv said, giving Sophia an uncertain expression.

She nodded. "We've allowed it all to go on this long. Another few days won't change much." She hoped she was right.

"Okay, that's good news," Alicia said, digging into a toolbox on the workstation. "I have something else for you, too."

Liv rubbed her hands together. "Isn't she great? Always supplying us with magitech gadgets? Last month she made me a device that puts people to sleep at the click of a button."

Alicia smiled. "Just don't use it on me and we're good."

"I'd love it if you used it on me," Sophia shared. "Falling asleep is difficult these days."

"Well, when you have the mission of saving the world, even counting sheep doesn't calm one's mind," Liv related.

"Especially if the sheep are all atheists," Sophia joked, earning confused expressions from the other two ladies. "Anyway, you have something for me?"

Alicia nodded, handing her a small black box. "That is a frequency regulator. I won't bore you with the details but—"

"Will you bore me with the details later?" Liv asked, eyeing the device with interest. Sophia's older sister had loved mortal electronics since the beginning, which parlayed into her initial career working at the electronics store for John Caraway. Later, when she had her magic unlocked and became a Warrior for the House of Fourteen, it was only natural for her interests to make her a magitech nut.

"You bet," Alicia answered before returning her attention to Sophia. "Now, this device can be your best friend or worst enemy, depending on how you use it."

"I'm intrigued," Liv said, leaning forward.

"If you're reliant on any magitech, then this will undermine your efforts," Alicia explained. "Fortunately, the compass I gave you won't be tampered with by you using this. However, if you are using any other magitech, it will make it ineffective."

"But the point is it will also bring down any of Thad Reinhart's magitech, right?" Sophia asked.

"That's the idea," Alicia agreed. "It sends out a frequency that should take the electronics offline, but depending on its level of power, it might just knock it out for a brief period. Hopefully, that's enough time to get you through a security measure or give you a way to figure out a strategy for combat."

Sophia eyed the device, holding it affectionately. "It's the best advantage we could ask for at this point since we have no idea what we're facing."

Liv clapped a solid hand on her shoulder, giving her sister a sturdy expression. "You may not know what you're facing, but I feel sorrier for the opposing side because they have no idea what's coming for them. You'll knock them out, Soph."

CHAPTER FORTY-TWO

"Point and shoot?" Wilder questioned. "That's what she said?"

Sophia nodded. "Yeah, Liv said there wasn't really anything to using the grappling hook. Just prepare to get hauled off my butt."

Wilder laughed. "Yeah, but if you don't know what you're doing, you can get hauled in all the wrong places."

The pair stood next to a rock wall on the far side of the Expanse, the Castle a backdrop to the training session. He patted his midsection. "When that grappling hook attaches to its target, you want to be prepared. If your core isn't engaged, the ride is going to be a bit uncomfortable, and the landing might rearrange your face, which would be a shame. It's key you're ready before you shoot. And then when it anchors, be ready and also when you land."

"Engage my core," Sophia repeated. "Cool, I can do that. It's like doing Pilates."

"What?" Wilder questioned.

"You know, Pilates?" she repeated. "The exercises you do on a reformer machine?"

He shook his head. "Is that a type of magic? What kind of spells does it call for?"

Sophia laughed. "Yoga pants and breath control. And no, it's not magic, unless having good posture and lean muscles is magic."

"It might be," Wilder pronounced. He positioned himself behind her, angling the hand holding the grappling hook at the rock wall. "Now, you want to be very precise with your aim, but also account for wind, temperature, air density, and any other factors that could throw it off."

"So, it's like golfing?" Sophia asked.

"Are all your references sports-related?" he questioned.

"Not all of them," she answered. "Sometimes they are pop culture, especially when I'm talking to Hiker because he doesn't get them and they make him angry."

"Angrier," Wilder corrected.

"Right," Sophia said, sandwiched in Wilder's arms as he held her hands with the grappling hook steady.

"Now, when you're ready, point and shoot," Wilder instructed.

"Engage core, account for variables, and get ready for a wild ride," Sophia said, listing the lessons she'd learned about grappling hooks.

He stood back and released her. "Oh, no. This is a wild ride. When you use that grappling hook, you're on your own."

"Ha-ha," she said, shaking her head at him. "That was an awful joke."

His dimples surfaced as he shrugged. "I make no apologies for bad jokes."

Sophia looked back over her shoulder at him, aware she wasn't focused on her target. "You really should." Then she pressed the trigger, holding steady as the grappling hook shot toward the wall. Not even turning around, she smiled as it hit its target and tugged her up to the top of the rock structure. When she neared it, Sophia turned and stuck her feet up to lock her into place just as she connected with the wall.

With a triumphant feeling pounding in her heart, she glanced down at Wilder with a proud smile. "How was that?"

"It was good, but you could have done it without showing off so much," he said.

"No, I couldn't have," she retorted.

When Sophia had lowered back down to the ground, Wilder showed her a few more techniques for using the grappling hook. "Now, after this whole Thad business, we'll have to take a break from your training for a bit."

"Because?" she questioned.

"Because I have to step away for a little while," he admitted, averting his eyes.

"Step away?" she asked. "That's what you have to do when you need to pop out for a cup of coffee or to run to the post office, but I get the impression there's more to this field trip you're planning."

"It's a mission for Subner," Wilder said in a low voice.

"Oh," she said with interest, putting her fist under her chin and regarding him with intense curiosity. "Let's share secrets."

He shook his head. "You know I can't. Subner asked for total confidentially with this one."

"But what if you need help?" Sophia questioned.

"From an eighteen-year-old dragonrider?" Wilder questioned with great skepticism.

Sophia scoffed. "How many days did you spend battling the dingoes in the Australian Outback?"

He sighed. "All of the days."

"Yeah, so don't underestimate youth," she said.

Wilder brushed long strands of hair off his shoulder rather dramatically. "Or beauty."

"Well, I won't pressure you about this secret mission with

Subner," Sophia stated. "Hopefully, I'm nearing the end of my training anyway."

"You are definitely close to earning your wings as a rider and making things official," Wilder agreed. "You should know training never ends for us. Hiker is adamant about that." He pushed out his chest and straightened, doing his best Hiker Wallace impression. "The world doesn't stop, and neither should we. Always be better than you were and the best you can be."

Sophia laughed, but honestly, she respected a motto like that. Hiker Wallace shouldn't be underestimated, and she hoped all his years of training would soon pay off for them. Earth was relying on it.

CHAPTER FORTY-THREE

Sophia was returning from training with Wilder when she spotted Quiet, once more suspiciously scampering across the Expanse, looking over his shoulder like he was worried he was being followed. Again, he was headed toward a large cluster of rocks by the Pond.

Having left Wilder on his own to do something mysterious he wouldn't elaborate on, Sophia found herself alone and in a perfect position to follow the gnome and find out once and for all what he was hiding. It was obvious everyone at the Gullington had their secrets, and Sophia's job was apparently to be a detective, unearthing them all.

She crouched and turned on her stealth mode so she could follow the groundskeeper. Moving soundlessly across the Expanse, she cleared the space easily, not spotted by Quiet.

He glanced over his shoulder in the opposite direction of where she was stationed before hurrying toward the rocks. She was so close. Finally, she'd see what he was up to.

"BRRRINGGGG!"

The ring of Sophia's cellphone echoed across the grounds,

making birds scatter from the field. Of course, the gnome turned with a scowl on his face, alerted to her presence.

Sophia blushed as she pulled the phone from her cloak pocket. It continued to ring, a rude sound that had not only given her away but was incessant and annoying.

"Hey," she said, putting the device to her ear, not recognizing the number. That was typical for magitech phones. Often those who didn't have her number could get it by using one.

"Hey there, cousin," said a voice on the other end of the line.

Not aware of any cousins out in the world, Sophia frowned. "Cousin? Who is this?"

"Don't you recognize my voice?" the person asked, and right then, Sophia did. She also knew this person wasn't related to her. They weren't even the same species. Or on the same wavelength.

"Hey, King Rudolf," she said mock-cheerfully. "How's it going? Did you lock yourself in a bathroom stall again? Maybe call Liv to get you out this time."

"I'm in a bathroom stall, but I can get out if I want to…I think," he replied. "Anyway, I'm just calling you to say the triplets are on their way, and I need you here pronto."

"Oh," she said, excitement filling her. "I'm thrilled you thought of me. I can't wait to meet your babies, but I'm actually on the brink of trying to stop a world war."

"That sounds like it can wait," Rudolf argued.

"You do understand what a world war is, right?" she questioned.

"You said 'brink,'" Rudolf reasoned. "That sounds like you have some time. Wait until all chaos spills over the waterfall and crashes to the bottom. That's when you swoop in. Don't you know anything about being a hero?"

Sophia shook her head. "Apparently, I don't."

"Well, I've been doing this for many, many centuries, so trust my advice," Rudolf yelled over a loud flushing sound. "Anyway, get here. I want you to meet my four children."

"Triplets," Sophia corrected. "You're having triplets."

"Exactly," he agreed. "Which is why I need you here. There will be one baby for each of us to hold while Serena rests after childbirth, which isn't a piece of cake, according to Bermuda Laurens. I'm guessing it's more like a walk in the park. Anyway, I've called Liv and Rory and now you. That means there will be a baby for each of us to care for, so get over here now."

"Okay," Sophia said, not having the heart to explain to Rudolf he was only having three children and didn't really need her since it felt good to be needed by someone. For a girl who only had two blood relatives in the world, it was nice to have so many people who felt like family. It just proved to Sophia that sometimes you have the family you were born to, and sometimes you have the family you choose.

CHAPTER FORTY-FOUR

"How did he take it?" Sophia asked when Liv returned from the delivery room, a speculative expression on her face.

She nodded. "The king of the fae seems relieved he's only having three babies."

Rory, the giant, shook his head. "You couldn't have told him this information prior to now?"

Liv laughed. "I didn't see you pony up any information to him."

Rory, whose subdued nature was a stark contrast to Liv's eccentric one, merely grunted. He was like Sophia's Hiker. She annoyed the Viking like Liv did Rory. It was as if it gave their life meaning to irritate a large grown man.

Maddy, Rory's girlfriend, had been called in to help with the birth since giants were considered very pragmatic on such occasions. It had to do with their magic being connected to the Earth. This left Sophia, Liv, and Rory ample time to stare blankly at each other.

The timing of the births couldn't have been better for Sophia to take some time off. She'd given Hiker the compass from Alicia, and that had started the forty-eight hour time period. She was hoping by the time she returned to the Gullington, the compass would be pointing them toward Thad Reinhart.

She could tell Hiker had mixed feelings about the whole thing. It had to be strange for him to be on the brink of confronting a great evil he was tied to. But he was the only one who could, and the time was quickly approaching. Worldwide events had heated up in the last twelve hours, tensions mounting between countries. War was inevitable for many.

"They are here!" Rudolf exclaimed, running from the labor and delivery room. He engulfed Liv in a hug and then Rory, who looked repulsed by the gesture, and then finally Sophia.

"They are healthy and have all eleven toes!" Rudolf declared.

"Eleven?" Liv questioned.

Rory shook his head. "All fae are born with eleven toes, but the weakest of them falls off later on."

Sophia grimaced. "That's so bizarre."

"The babies are healthy, though?" Liv asked, appearing sentimental. "That's great news, Rudolf."

"Yeah, and we can go through to the nursery in just a minute and hold them," he explained, but then tucked his chin and leaned forward, cupping his mouth. "I'm going to warn you, they are awful-looking."

Liv's eyes slid to Sophia and she had a cautious expression on her face. "Do fae children look like monsters when they are born?"

Rory shook his head.

"Oh, yes, they do," Rudolf argued. "Their faces are all pinched and red, and they look like old men. It's like they were crammed in a tiny compartment for a long time."

"So weird," Sophia said with no inflection.

"They don't do much," Rudolf said, leading them to another set of doors and looking over his shoulder at them. "Bermuda says they will probably just sleep for a long time."

"What were you expecting?" Liv dared to ask.

He shrugged, opening the door. "I had planned a snowshoeing excursion, as well as some paddle boarding for next week, but they apparently can't walk for like a year. I question that, though. Is it that they can't, or they aren't trying hard enough?"

"Maybe with that extra toe, they'll defy the odds," Sophia offered.

Three bassinets were lined up in a room adjacent to the birthing facility. In each of the beds was a tiny baby with a hat on its head, all wrapped up. All that could be seen were pinched red faces.

"Please allow me to introduce you to my girls," Rudolf said proudly.

"They are all girls?" Liv asked, sounding excited.

Rudolf nodded. "Yeah, although they can change their mind at any point. But for now, we'll refer to them as girls."

He picked up the first one, who had a round face and wide eyes and her hand in her mouth. "This one is my firstborn and she is hungrier than most, according to Bermuda. She's a Capricorn, and we named her Captain Morgan." He handed the bundle to Liv, who hesitated at first, but after some trials, she slipped her hands around the baby and cuddled her to her chest.

"Hi, Morgan," she said, a strange tenderness taking residence on her face. "I'm your godmother, and I promise to teach you everything your parents haven't picked up through sheer experience. I'm going to keep you alive, little one."

Rudolf watched this exchange with affection before turning his attention to the middle bassinet. He picked up a bundle that was longer than the other two. This child's face was slender, although red.

"And now, may I present my second child, who Bermuda says came out the wrong way, but that's better than not coming out at all. She's a Taurus named Captain Silver."

"How is it she's a Taurus if they were all born on the same day of the same month?" Liv asked, bouncing her baby.

Rudolf shook his head as he handed the baby to Rory, who seemed quite natural holding the bundle. "It's a decision they make. Our zodiacs don't choose us, we choose them."

"That's inherently false," Sophia said, watching as Rory thoughtfully gazed down at the baby and made her coo.

Rudolf pivoted and pulled the third baby from the last bed. "And here is my last-born baby, who Bermuda said didn't want to come out. She's stubborn, clever, and probably my favorite. Please meet Captain Kirk." He laid the baby in Sophia's arms, and for never having held a child before, she found the experience to be quite natural. The baby cuddled into her, its warmth a welcome sensation in a world where Sophia was used to so much cold.

"I don't think you're supposed to have favorites yet," Liv offered, gazing down at her baby with affection.

Rudolf waved her off, dismissing her comment. "Of course, I am. That's how I pit them against one another, so they work harder to achieve their father's approval, which never comes."

"Smart parenting," Rory said. "That won't fail."

Rudolf was absolutely giddy, bouncing between the three holding his children, commenting on their different characteristics, or making assumptions about their political affiliations.

He came around to Sophia and peered over her shoulder, fondly regarding the baby in her arms, who was fast asleep.

"If there is a world war coming, Sophia, will you do everything possible to stop it?" Rudolf asked, his voice suddenly serious. "I brought these girls into the world. They are quite possibly the first half-fae and half-mortal children ever. I want a legacy for them that is deserving of their greatness. I want them to rule in a world that is appreciative of their uniqueness. And I want them to thrive on an Earth that is both beautiful and conducive to their growth. Will you help me to secure that future for the Captains?"

As looney as King Rudolf Sweetwater always was, he was also

one of the best people Sophia had the fortune of meeting. He might get a lot of things wrong, but he got many more right, and the three brand new halflings in the nursery were part of that. King Rudolf was someone worth knowing and protecting, and his girls were reason enough to ensure war didn't take over the Earth.

"Yes, Ru," Sophia answered thoughtfully, handing Captain Kirk back to her father. "I'll go fight the bad guys so one day these girls will know a peaceful Earth."

CHAPTER FORTY-FIVE

When Sophia returned to the Gullington, her heart was full of love and a need to protect future generations. And because her life had to be ironic, she was greeted by screaming upon entering the Castle.

"We've got to act now!" Hiker yelled from his office.

Sophia hurried up the stairs to the second story, rushing into his office to find a similar scene as before. Mama Jamba was laid out on the couch, still watching movies, and Hiker was pacing.

"I know that, Hiker," Mama Jamba stated. "The situation has been horrible since the beginning. I'm glad you're finally taking note of it."

He looked at the magitech device Sophia had given him. "The compass still isn't registering Thad's location."

"It will," Mama Jamba said in her drawn-out accent. "When it's time."

"Mama!" he boomed, throwing his hand at a television screen in the corner. "The reports are saying countries are moving into position. Armies are gearing up. Within the day, shots are supposed to be fired, all because of this fake need for resources and power Thad has brainwashed them with. He's pitted those with pitchforks against those with torches and told them they are each other's enemy."

Mama Jamba nodded calmly, pulling a warm afghan up to her chin and cuddling it. "Yes, that's exactly what he's done. He wants the world's population to take each other out, and in the process, kill the Earth. And he might be successful." She toggled her head back and forth. "But he also might not."

The two hadn't noticed Sophia lurking in the doorway. When she cleared her throat, they both turned their attention to her.

"You're back," Hiker said.

"Yes, sir," she answered. "Is everything…"

He shook his head. "No, it's not okay, but hopefully, it will be. Get ready to mobilize. The others are also preparing. I want you to be ready to go at a moment's notice. As soon as this thing you've given me shows Thad's location and facility, we're off."

Sophia nodded, adrenaline suddenly coursing through her veins. They were almost to it. The moment had almost come. And it was no greater for anyone than Hiker Wallace. Soon his moment of reckoning would be upon them. For Sophia, she wasn't sure whether he'd redeem himself from all those centuries ago when he let Thad get away or if he'd repeat the past.

CHAPTER FORTY-SIX

E veryone was silent, on the verge of panic when they all seemed to get a phone call from within.

Mama Jamba hiccupped like she'd swallowed something the wrong way and pressed her hand to her mouth. Hiker's eyes fell distant, the way Sophia imagined hers did when Lunis spoke in her head. Then her dragon did speak.

I think you better come here and see this, Lunis said, his tone tense.

What is it? Sophia asked.

It's better if you see this on your own rather than hear it from me, Lunis insisted. *But bring Hiker.*

He's getting a message from Bell right now, I think, Sophia replied.

Yes, that seems about right, Lunis stated.

Sophia's and Hiker's eyes met, and they shared a foreboding expression.

Okay, we are on our way, Sophia told the dragon. *But first, is everything okay?*

"Okay" is always relative, Soph, he explained. *There's status quo, and then there's the precipitance to evolution, and then there's the oppo-*

site of all that. I hope we're somewhere in the middle, but only time will tell.

Sophia and Hiker crossed the Expanse in silence. They hadn't said a word to each other when they left the Castle, both knowing their dragons had communicated similar messages.

As they neared the Cave, the tension mounted in Sophia's chest. She had to take three steps to one of Hiker's. She moved faster than him, so it worked out.

When they were at the bottom of the mountain that housed the Cave, they both halted.

"I've never been up to the Cave," Sophia admitted.

Hiker shook his head. "Me either. But if the dragons are asking us to enter, this is big."

"And Bell didn't tell you what it was about?" Sophia questioned, knowing his dragon had spoken in his head at the same time Lunis had in her mind.

"No, she said I had to see it in person," he stated.

Sophia nodded. "Same with Lunis." She motioned to the rock wall. "We can climb or use my awesome grappling hook."

To her surprise, Hiker rolled his eyes. "Awesome grappling hook, obviously."

She nodded and pulled it off her belt.

The Cave had never had humans in it. Sophia had seen it in Lunis' mind when she'd scried his visions. However, no person had ever stepped foot in the Cave, which had been the home of dragons since the beginning of the Gullington, the beginning of the Dragon Elite.

It felt like stepping onto a brand-new uninhabited planet

when Sophia entered the Cave. Hiker seemed to share her anxiety. The dragons, if they felt anything about the trespassing, didn't show it.

Sophia knew with her first glance at Lunis that something was devastatingly wrong. It gave her little chance to notice the details of the Cave. It was nondescript, as she knew from scrying. There were cold, dark walls and little light. The ground was hard and unforgiving, as Lunis had often told her. In the corner were the shimmering dragon eggs she and Evan had recovered from one of Thad's facilities, but unlike the last time she'd seen them, they weren't shimmering.

CHAPTER FORTY-SEVEN

Sophia rushed over and knelt beside the five dragons who surrounded the eggs nestled in the corner. Hiker didn't follow.

She glanced at him, and her heart broke.

Sophia almost didn't have to look at the eggs to know what had happened. It was plainly written all over Hiker Wallace's face.

They had gone bad.

She pulled her gaze around to the five eggs and looked them over.

That's when she noticed cracks running down their sides and saw they were shrinking in on themselves. They were withering away.

"What happened?" she asked Lunis, sidling up next to him.

He shook his head. *We don't know.*

They could have always been bad, Coral answered, sitting next to Lunis.

It was strange to Sophia that the dragons all sitting around the eggs seemed more like housecats than large reptiles. Maybe it was just the significance of the moment.

"Lunis came from this batch," Sophia argued.

We all came from the same batch, Bell stated. *It's just that we were separated.*

One thousand eggs, Tala said stoically.

"And the very last five are dead," Hiker stated, sounding more like a zombie than himself. He ambled forward robotically, his eyes on the eggs. "The last of the dragons. Our very last hope. It's gone."

Sophia felt emotion welling up in her, but she refused to let it out in front of ancient dragons and the oldest rider. Instead, she swallowed. "But still, sir, a few remain."

He shook his head, pulling his gaze away as he turned for the entrance. "What does that matter anymore? There are only a handful of us left, and we are hardly enough. Our numbers were always our strong point."

"That's wrong," Sophia declared, not sure where her words were coming from. "Our power has always been in our unity. Mortals are powerful because of their grasp on magic. Elves with water. Gnomes, their ability with fire. And giants own the Earth. But only one race has ever dared to pair their grasp of wind and magic with that of the dragon. We are magicians, and we were chosen to ride. There is no lost hope as long as one of us breathes in this world."

Sophia took a step forward. "Sir, I'm breathing. Are you?"

She watched as Hiker's back rose and fell, the stress of the moment getting to him. Finally, he turned, a sober look in his eyes. He nodded. "Yes, Sophia. I'm breathing too."

She pointed behind her. "So are these dragons. They may be all that's left, but they are enough for us to win at least one more battle. One more war. Will you lead us into it?"

Hiker pulled in a breath, seeming on the verge of answering, but something pulsed in his pocket. He tensed and retrieved the compass. His eyes widened before he brought his gaze up.

"I know where Thad is," he said in a hushed voice.

"But are you ready?" she asked, feeling the dragons at her back, their strength fueling her in a way she'd never felt before.

He lowered the compass and nodded, his eyes darting to the dead eggs before landing on Sophia. "Unlike before, I have nothing to lose and everything to gain."

CHAPTER FORTY-EIGHT

Even after hiking around the Expanse for several hours, Sophia was having trouble processing what she'd just learned about the dragon eggs. Yes, there were only five before. That had given the riders a little hope the Dragon Elite would be what it once was, although no one voiced it aloud. Having five eggs was better than nothing.

They knew because Mae Ling had confirmed it, that these were the last five remaining eggs in the world. Knowing they would never hatch and there would never be another new dragon was devastating no matter how Sophia tried to spin it. Yes, there were still five dragons left in the world, and barring tragedy, they could live a thousand or more years. But after that, the age of the dragons would be gone. The Dragon Elite would be no more. The world adjudicators would be done.

Sophia tried to console herself with the fact Lunis came from that batch of eggs, and at least he hatched. Who knew why the dragon eggs went bad? The dragons had speculated it might have been the approaching war. It was triggering all sorts of things worldwide.

Bermuda thought the war was the reason King Rudolf Sweetwater's children were born when they were. Apparently, global consciousness was affected by the events Thad had put into motion, and it had far-reaching effects.

Still consumed with these thoughts, Sophia trudged up the stairs to the Castle, hoping to get a proper night's rest. Tomorrow the war was coming. The Dragon Elite would ride out together for the first time in centuries.

Sophia wasn't overwhelmed by what would come next, but she was preoccupied with it. That was why she didn't hear Mama Jamba call to her as she walked past Hiker's office.

The suit of armor stationed in the corridor stepped out from the wall and pointed at Sophia's back. Not as surprised as she should have been that empty armor was walking around by itself, she glanced over her shoulder, realizing the Castle was trying to communicate with her.

"Get your hiney in here, darling," Mama Jamba called from the open office.

"Oh, right," Sophia said, turning back to the suit of armor and nodding. "Thanks."

Pivoting, she hurried back the way she'd come. She'd just thanked an empty suit of armor for giving her directions. "My life is so weird."

"It will only get weirder," Mama Jamba said, still stationed on Hiker's couch. He was absent from his office, probably helping the dragons to dispose of the bad eggs.

Mother Nature appeared refreshed in comparison to her recent appearance. There were no wadded up tissues scattered around her, and she'd changed into a fresh pink velour tracksuit. Her silver hair was neatly arranged, and her feet were covered in sparkling Ugg boots that matched her outfit.

"I'm guessing you know about..." Sophia's voice trailed away.

Mama Jamba nodded and patted the space beside her on the couch. "Of course, I do, my dear. You must be taking this hard."

Sophia took the spot beside Mother Nature and nodded. "Did you always know they were going to spoil?"

Mama pulled in a breath and clasped her hands over her midsection. "The thing is, there isn't really such thing as destiny, and yet there is."

Sophia hung her head. "That doesn't make any sense."

Mama Jamba nodded. "And yet, that's the way life goes."

"Why does life have to be so complicated?" Sophia asked.

"Because there are no absolutes," Mama Jamba stated. "I made most of the rules. Papa made quite a few as well. And we made them, so they were never hard and fast. Each one can be broken if you know the secret, but…" She winked at Sophia, a twinkle in her bright blue eyes. "We don't give up our secrets easily."

"No, I wouldn't think you would," Sophia offered.

"So," Mama Jamba continued, "the eggs were meant to hatch, but things changed. And now they're spoiled. There is destiny, and it can always shift."

"Then it's not destiny," Sophia argued.

Mama Jamba agreed. "I understand how confusing this is, this game of semantics if you will. You're destined for certain things, and you will fulfill that destiny, most likely. But if you leave this room and an axe falls on you, then you won't."

"Well, the Castle has tried to kill me before," Sophia muttered.

Mama Jamba laughed. "It was simply trying to steer you in the direction it desired. My point is, events change what was destined. And now the eggs won't hatch."

"And that's the end of dragons," Sophia said.

"Not quite." Mama Jamba patted her leg. "We still have you."

"I finished the meditative portion of my training," Sophia said. "Does that mean I'm done? Do I have my wings?"

Mama Jamba smiled. "Almost. I knew you'd wrap it up quickly, and I'm grateful you're almost there. However, you have one last thing to do before you officially pass."

"Travel to another planet?" Sophia asked. "Survive a walkabout in the Australian Outback? Not kill Hiker after he throws away my provisions and demands I hike ten miles? Oh, wait, I've already done all those things."

The laugh that spilled from Mama Jamba's mouth was absolutely enchanting. It was the sound of the wind rustling willow branches. "Actually, the last task you must complete to finish training isn't something you can go out and do."

"Seems about right," Sophia said dryly.

"Instead, you're waiting for an opportunity," Mama Jamba continued. "To earn your wings, you must show a true act of comradery."

"How do I do that?" Sophia asked.

The old woman shook her head. "That will be for you to determine. I will say that if you go out looking for a way, it won't count. When we try to be nice, we're using the wrong motivation. When it comes from the purest part of the heart and we express love because it calls to us, then that is magic."

"A true act of comradery…" Sophia mused, her eyes looking without seeing.

"Yes, because that's the biggest part of being with the Dragon Elite," Mama Jamba explained. "They protect the world because they value life, and no lives are more important to my Elite than the other riders'."

"So I have to show an act of comradery to one of the riders," Sophia stated.

"Again, it has to be authentic and unplanned," Mama Jamba warned.

"I did tell you I didn't murder Hiker even though he was all but begging me to, right?" Sophia joked.

"I appreciate that, but I'm afraid that won't do." Mama patted her leg once more. "You'll figure it out, my dear. Or you won't and it will take you several years to complete your training, like Evan."

"But you told me completing the training is crucial," Sophia argued, remembering how adamant the woman had been about it.

"Indeed, I did, and it is. But so were a lot of other things that haven't happened in history," she explained. "Unfortunately, bad things happen, and usually that's a result of other things *not* happening. If you don't complete your training in time, I fear for this world, but I already do, so it's just more of the same."

Sophia fell quiet for a moment, trying not to feel overwhelmed by all this. After a moment, she pointed to the television screen before them on the table in front of the couch. "Are you done with sad movies?"

The television was blank, showing just static.

Mama Jamba smiled good-naturedly as she nodded. "Yes. How about you and I watch something that will make you laugh? You seem like you could use it."

"I could," Sophia related. "What do you want to watch?"

"Well, I don't know," Mama Jamba said, yarn and a crochet hook appearing in her hands. She immediately went to work making something. She held it up. "For one of King Rudolf's triplets."

"Oh, wow, they get a baby blanket from Mother Nature? Is it because their father is the king of the fae?"

"Everyone gets something from me," Mama Jamba answered. "They just don't always know it. This is because the triplets are unique."

"Because they are halflings?" Sophia asked.

In response, Mother Nature bobbed her head. "And other reasons, too, but no spoilers for you."

"And destiny could change," Sophia added.

Indicating the screen, Mama Jamba said, "Now, pick something to watch. You probably know all the hip new shows all the kids are watching? Is there something on Prime or Netflix I need to see?"

Sophia blinked at the woman. "Why do you not know everything? I'm confused by how this works."

"As you should be. It's very confusing. I know most things, but not everything. Like Papa Creola, I see the future, but not all of it. I can control many things, but only under the right circumstances, and all of that is subject to change if certain rules are broken."

"Wow," Sophia said, shaking her head. "Okay, well, how about some Trey Kennedy?"

"Oh, he's delightful," Mama Jamba stated at once.

"You've seen his YouTube channel?" Sophia asked.

Mother Nature shook her head. "No, I just know everyone."

"Right," Sophia said, pointing at the television and making YouTube pop up on the screen.

"Now, what does he do?" Mama Jamba asked, continuing to crochet the blanket.

"He does these spoofs where he makes fun of people: single girls, middle schoolers, white people, adults, millennials, people in the winter, moms. You know, that sort of thing?" Sophia explained. "It's like the stereotypical behavior we all are prone to, but he calls it out, making it funny."

"Oh, something like how moms be like 'Kids, get mommy one of her Dove dark chocolates,' or 'What is this Sea World? How is there so much water outside the tub?' or 'How do I send a G-I-F?' or 'Good morning, or should I say, good afternoon. Someone slept well,' or 'Put your coat on and take your other one. You never know,' or 'How was your pool party? Were the girls wearing appropriate swimsuits?'"

Sophia peeled back, giving Mama Jamba a look of astonishment. "Yeah, that was pretty much the episode on moms verbatim."

Mama Jamba scrunched her shoulders, looking proud. "I gave him some of my best jokes. Love that kid."

CHAPTER FORTY-NINE

Sophia sat atop Lunis, her fingers on the reins and her attention on Hiker Wallace as he did what he did best—pace. He strode in front of the line of dragons on the Expanse, thinking. She'd grown accustomed to seeing him pace. Fret. Worry away his thoughts.

She looked around, taking in the green hills and capturing the picture around her. It was unlike anything she'd ever seen, but she hoped to see it more often in the future. Four dragons with their riders atop them stood at the ready. In front of them, Hiker, the leader of the Dragon Elite, paced along the Expanse, his red dragon standing nobly at his back.

On the far side next to Evan stood Ainsley and Quiet, serious expressions on both their faces.

These five riders were all that remained of the Dragon Elite. After a thousand years and some odd, there were only five left with dragons. And then there was Thad Reinhart, the worst of the worst and the one they had to take down.

He didn't have a dragon. Thad had something worse. He had perfected magitech and turned it into his dragon. Sophia knew planes and jets enhanced with magitech and all other things related to the modern world would come at her that day. It would be the worst battle she'd ever endured.

As she looked at Wilder atop Simi on her right, she nodded. Mahkah sat upon Tala on her left, and he gave her confidence. They were all the Earth had, and it had to be enough.

Hiker paced some more before halting. Clearing his throat, he looked at his riders.

"I haven't always been the leader you wanted," he began. "But I have always tried to be the one you needed. I looked out for the dangers, but I missed them because I didn't know they were within me. Thad is my problem. He is the result of what I couldn't finish."

Hiker seemed on the verge of having a moment as he sped up, moving faster with his words, almost like he was still pacing in his thoughts.

"I have been a dragonrider since before any of you were born, but I've learned our years mean nothing." His eyes darted to Sophia. "I've learned wisdom comes from listening." His gaze darted to Mahkah. "I've learned experience comes from sacrifice." His eyes moved to Wilder. "I've learned positions come to those who go through hell and back." And finally, his eyes went to Evan. "And I've learned ingenuity comes to those who challenge the world around them."

He moved until he was right in front of Bell. "You all have stayed by me, some of you longer than others, showing your loyalty. That has always been appreciated. I know you're waiting for the fight. It is here and it wants us, and it will not be done until we are done. Men…riders," he corrected. "We have spent a long time waiting to be needed, and our time is here."

Hiker mounted his dragon in an easy series of movements that brought him up on the large red magical creature.

"I can't thank you enough for staying true to me," he stated, holding Bell's reins. "However, I have one more request, and it's probably the hardest one yet."

Hiker looked each of them in the eye before gazing at Bell. "If all else fails, if I don't succeed, elect a leader of the Dragon Elite who will keep you honest until the end."

"That's your request?" Ainsley asked, holding up a basket. "I have muffins. Does anyone want muffins for the journey?"

Hiker shook his head. "Would you get out of here, woman? We are having a moment."

Ainsley pointed at Quiet standing close by. "He said it was all right to interrupt and your speech was drivel and I should offer muffins to soften the boring part."

Hiker shook his head. "I'm trying to rally my men. People. Riders."

She shook her head. "No, you're boring them. If I was giving a speech, it would go something like—"

"You're fired, Ainsley," Hiker said flatly.

She bowed. "It is about time, sir. I've been waiting for this moment. I'll see you when you return."

He nodded. "See you later."

She turned and headed for the Castle in the distance.

Quiet also muttered something before ambling off, leaving the riders and their leader staring around blankly.

Sophia sensed they were all waiting for that "Braveheart" moment, and they might not get it. She smiled at Hiker and mouthed the words, "You've got this."

He smiled. Tightening his hands on the reins, he led his dragon in front of them. Bell moved with unique grace, striding back and forth as if she were pacing like her rider.

"I'm sorry if I have faltered," Hiker began, his voice stronger than before. "But follow me into battle, and we will not fail. I will fight Thad. You will take down his arsenal. And we will show our rule once more over this Earth. Even if we are the last of the dragonriders, we will be the very best this planet has ever known."

CHAPTER FIFTY

The dragons rose, their wings flapping in perfect unison. Hiker was in the lead, directing his riders outside the Barrier, where he'd open a portal close to Thad's facility.

The Dragon Elite rode in formation, Evan and Sophia bringing up the rear. The sun was just rising over the Gullington, but where they were headed, it would still be night, which was important for their plan.

In truth, none of them knew exactly what they'd face. They could have taken time to do reconnaissance on the area, but Hiker had said it was time to act. There would be weapons. Fighting. Resistance. They were aware of that, and it was as much preparation as they needed.

Sophia had never ridden among the other riders like this, watching the tails of the dragons stream behind them in the wind. She felt a rush of emotion, her mind trailing back to ancient memories that weren't hers. In a flash, she saw Hiker riding next to Adam, the wind ripping through their hair and beards as they raced through a torrential rainstorm. She saw battles where intertwined dragons plummeted toward the ground. She saw the first rider, Alexander Conerly, flying over a clear blue ocean.

It's the chi of the dragon, Lunis said in her head. *It's connecting you to the memories of other riders like I am often connected to the collective consciousness of dragons.*

Wow, I didn't realize that was possible, Sophia said.

Anything is possible, Lunis said simply. *You're embarking on a pivotal adventure, and this is your first time to ride alongside the Dragon Elite. It's triggered memories of your own.*

Sophia was speechless, feeling the ancient winds the riders who came before her had felt. She felt the power of the dragons around her, a collective power that sent out a frequency unlike anything she'd known.

At that moment, she was connected to the past and the present of the Dragon Elite. The power of her own flowed around like the wind, and she made peace with the element that had always made her shrink in on herself.

She felt the blast of cold and didn't even consider hunching over to avoid the wind. Instead, Sophia straightened on Lunis, drinking in the breeze and holding her face high. She braced her shoulders and rode into the wind alongside the other Dragon Elite, for the first time feeling like one of them.

CHAPTER FIFTY-ONE

S ophia was the last to come through the portal, coasting in
over the flat and sprawling city of Dallas, Texas.

The skyline was lit up, blotting out the stars. The moon hung
overhead, a giant full orb high in the Texas sky.

Did you know it was a full moon? Sophia asked her dragon,
having been too preoccupied recently to have made note of such
things.

Of course, I did, Lunis replied. *I can feel them approach.*

That will make things interesting tonight, Sophia offered.

It will give me certain advantages, Lunis stated. *I'm both strongest
and most vulnerable on the full moon.*

How is that possible?

That's how it is with most things, he explained. *A bodybuilder bulks
up to be stronger, but it also makes them a bigger target.*

Right, Sophia replied. *If you turn on your supersize skills, we'll
have benefits, but you'll be a larger target.*

Exactly.

The pollution that hung over the city was a stark contrast to
the clean air Sophia was used to in the Gullington. The city of
Dallas was filled with rows of cookie-cutter houses and roads,

planned out on a mass scale. Buildings and bright lights stretched around the highways, where traffic moved sluggishly along, commuters headed home after a long workday.

Hiker spun the compass in his hand, and a confused expression appeared in his eyes. He pointed to Sophia and waved her forward.

"Why her, sir?" Evan complained from beside her.

"Because," Hiker yelled.

Sophia clenched her heels tighter to Lunis as he sped up and navigated between Mahkah and Wilder. The pair slowed, making room for her as she pulled up next to the leader of the Dragon Elite.

"The compass shows we're right on top of his facility," Hiker explained to her, the wind tangling his words. She made them out, thanks to her enhanced senses.

Sophia glanced down to find the city had abruptly stopped. Pastures dotted with trees spread out in front of them. It was possible Thad Reinhart lived in a modest cabin on a farm on the outskirts of the city, but knowing what she did about the man, it seemed unlikely. This compass wasn't just taking them to Thad Reinhart. It was also drawing them to a huge source of magitech energy.

A mostly empty series of pastures definitely wasn't the spot for magitech power. Yes, magical power, but to have magitech, there *had* to be technology. There was no getting around that.

"Did Thad know about the Barrier at the Gullington?" Sophia asked.

A perplexed expression crossed Hiker's face. "Well, of course. Early on, I tried to recruit him for the Dragon Elite, shortly after I magnetized to Bell and him to Ember. I thought being a rider might change him." He shook his head, obviously disappointed. "I was naïve then."

Sophia withdrew the frequency disk Alicia had given her

from her pocket. "I think it's possible Thad created something similar to what we have at the Gullington."

"The Barrier," Hiker stated. "So his facility can't be seen or found by those who aren't welcome."

"And they also wouldn't be able to enter," Sophia said, slowing the dragon.

Hiker followed suit, as did the other riders at their backs, until they were all hovering over the field, the dragons flapping their wings to keep them aloft.

"If that's the case, how are we going to get in there?" Hiker asked.

"The Barrier keeps out anyone who isn't a Dragon Elite or serving them," Sophia explained. "However, Thad couldn't have the same parameters, I don't think. His would be controlled by magitech."

She set the controls on the frequency disk the way Alicia had shown her. Hiker watched curiously.

"If this works, sir, it will only bring down the security for a moment," Sophia explained. "That will be our chance to slip through. If it doesn't work, we have to find another way."

He nodded. "Then let's hope it works."

Sophia turned a dial on the disk and held her breath as the red meter on the front rose, showing it powering up and disturbing outside magitech frequencies. It wasn't choosey according to Alicia, so it would put all magitech offline for a brief period. The longer it was on, the more it could do, but stronger devices would resist after a short time.

It was lucky for the Dragon Elite they weren't reliant on magitech; otherwise, it could bring them down too. The compass was magitech, but it had already gotten them to their destination. Now they had to pull the disguise off of the facility.

"Here we go," Sophia said, watching as the meter rose all the way.

Hiker searched the area below them, his eyes anxious.

She flicked her eyes from the meter to the dark pastures, worried it wouldn't work.

Then, like Christmas lights flickering on for the first time in a season, a giant base materialized below them, spreading out a great distance.

Hiker let out a sound of shock. "For the love of the angels!"

CHAPTER FIFTY-TWO

The main headquarters of Thad Reinhart's enterprises wasn't like the Chainley facility Sophia and Lunis had visited, where they'd freed the slaves. That was tiny compared to this.

This was like a small city or a large military base. The tarmac stretched on, surrounded by lakes and irrigation ditches. Dotting the asphalt were dozens of jets, 747 planes, tanks, army jeeps mounted with guns, and semi-trucks. On the north end of the facility were multiple buildings and large warehouses, and in the center was an impressive fifty-story skyscraper. Without magitech, there was little way Thad Reinhart could have shielded this place.

The Gullington was hidden, but that was by an ancient and mysterious power fueled by whatever controlled the Castle. The House of Fourteen was similar, but it was fueled by the power of the founding families.

As far as Sophia knew, Thad Reinhart didn't have access to that level of magic. Technology was his strong point, and he'd fused it with magic to create a very impressive arsenal of magitech and security measures.

The base flickered below them like a lightbulb about to burn out.

"We have to go now," Sophia urged, waving those behind her forward.

Hiker sent Bell into a nosedive, and her large form took on the shape of a missile as it raced toward the ground. The others followed as the barrier to the military base began to fade. They had to get through before it did since Sophia wasn't sure she could get it to come back using the frequency disk. Bringing it down for this long had been a stroke of luck since whatever fueled it had to be a huge source of energy.

Alicia had also advised Sophia that magitech was intuitive and learned. A really advanced system taken offline by something will patch itself until it figures out how to troubleshoot the problem for the future.

Alicia had explained this to her to caution Sophia not to use the frequency disk too often. If she did, then when she really needed it, it might not work. For example, use it to bring down a helicopter, and it might be ineffective on the fighter jets they fought later.

The Dragon Elite raced toward the base. When Sophia slipped through the magitech barrier, she felt a force like static electricity run over her and Lunis. She halted in the air beside Hiker after they were all through the barrier.

The force field seemed to have affected them all. Hiker's long blond hair was sticking straight up like he'd had a balloon rubbed all over it.

Sophia laughed, relieved by having made it to their destination.

"What are you laughing at?" Hiker asked, sitting nobly upon his ancient dragon.

She pointed at his hair, which was reaching for the clouds. "You look funny."

CHAPTER FIFTY-THREE

W ith an annoyed glare, Hiker ran his hands through his hair, making it calm down once more. "You should see yours if you think mine looks funny."

Sophia could feel her hair wiggling all around her like it was possessed.

The other riders pulled up next to them, Wilder's head of brown hair also crazy from the static electricity.

"Anyone else keep shocking their dragon?" Evan asked, sidling up next to Mahkah.

I think the question you have to ask yourself, Lunis began, *is why does your dragon keep shocking you?*

Simi nodded, smiling at Lunis. *Yeah, I absorbed all of the electrical force I could so as not to jolt my rider.*

Me too, Tala admitted.

Evan bent and gazed at Coral. "Are you shocking me on purpose?"

Maybe? his dragon answered.

Hiker, who was not paying attention to this exchange, had his attention hinged on the military base below them. It had appeared to be mostly quiet at this time in the evening.

Sophia had actually thought it would be easy to drop in and scout around the place. Things were quickly changing below as fighter pilots ran to their jets and soldiers were deployed to the tanks and jeeps. They had triggered an alarm when they came through the barrier, and they were about to have a fight on their hands.

"We came to fight, though," Sophia said mostly to herself.

"That we did," Hiker replied, watching with keen interest as things quickly took shape on the ground.

Men in uniform scattered quickly, more spilling from the large adjacent buildings. There were a few dozen of them. She didn't have to remind herself there were only five of them. But they had dragons, and they had each other. It had to be enough.

Sophia was looking at Hiker, waiting for his orders as his jaw flexed and an expression of pure vengeance she'd never seen flickered in his eyes. Following his gaze, she saw what had caused the bitter expression.

A man in a black suit with a bald head and a face covered in scars had come out of the largest warehouse. Her enhanced vision studied the details of the man on the ground, who was different from the others racing towards aircraft or vehicles. She recognized his confidence. It was much like that of the man next to her. However, there was something so inherently evil about the man it radiated from even that distance.

He narrowed his gaze on the five dragonriders.

Thad Reinhart knew they were there. It was time for battle.

CHAPTER FIFTY-FOUR

Sophia cut her eyes to Hiker as he stayed locked on his twin brother on the ground. She watched him for signs of defeat. Everything centered on Hiker Wallace remaining confident in this battle. If he didn't, everything was lost. All the wars Thad Reinhart had instigated would commence. All the things they didn't want to come to pass would sprint forward. Hiker had to be what stopped his brother in order to stop everything that would destroy the planet.

The pair stared at each other for a long minute before Thad Reinhart pivoted sharply and strode back to the building he'd come from and disappeared. On the ground, the jets and vehicles were deploying. The fight was coming.

Drawing in a breath, Hiker dispersed orders at once. "We first have to take down the most vital offensive forces." He pointed to the ground where a large plane was sitting on the tarmac, a ground crew quickly fueling it. "That right there has something aboard it Thad doesn't want to be compromised."

"How do you know, sir?" Evan asked.

Hiker glanced back at him. "I know. Thad isn't used to me being close. He wasn't guarded just now, and I spied enough."

Indicating the jets taking off, Hiker said, "Mahkah and Wilder, you immobilize the small aircraft." He pointed at the tanks and jeeps moving into position. "Evan, you will draw the ground transport over to the water on the far edge. From there, you'll know what to do."

"Drown those frockers," Evan sang.

Sophia laughed, remembering Coral was aligned with water. That also reminded her of the others' elements. Simi was connected to the wind and Tala to the Earth. She wasn't sure how that would come into play or if it would, but she hoped they used every advantage they had in this fight.

Finally, when she thought Hiker had forgotten about her, he turned his attention to Sophia. "That plane. Thad referred to it in his mind as a 747. I want you and Lunis to take it down. Don't let whatever is aboard leave this facility."

She nodded, feeling the weight of great responsibility on her and Lunis' shoulders. "Yes, sir."

He leaned forward. "And my job will be to draw my brother out as only I can."

"How will you do that, sir?" Evan asked.

Hiker didn't give him a look of annoyance as Sophia would have expected. Instead, he drew a breath and sat up straighter. "It won't be hard. I don't know what Thad has, but he's excited to show it off to me. I think it is only a matter of time before my brother comes out of hiding, and I will be ready."

Sophia desperately hoped Hiker was right, and he was finally ready to face his twin.

CHAPTER FIFTY-FIVE

Because Wilder and Mahkah had a few dozen decades together, they shared a unique communication style.

He knew Mahkah would handle the aircraft being deployed, while Wilder was in charge of those already in the air.

The jets took off before turning around and coming in his and Simi's direction. He patted his dragon, encouraging her as they entered into their first real twenty-first-century battle.

Jets weren't something Wilder was familiar with. However, he was going to venture that they didn't know how to react to a dragon and rider. Most importantly, the jets had no idea what aces the dragonriders had up their sleeves.

Six jets roared in their direction, quickly approaching.

Wilder drew a breath, feeling his dragon suck in the wind like she was swallowing it and funneling it into a reserve. It was rare he and Simi had an opportunity to use their elemental skill. Actually, it had been forever.

This was their first real battle.

Long-awaited and with high stakes.

Most of the jets and aircraft were still on the ground, Mahkah observed, directing Tala over them.

He'd only have one chance to strike. After that, Tala would be depleted. He would have to channel all his power into one move instead of splitting it up. The key was to keep the other aircraft from taking off.

Unfortunately, the 747 with the important cargo was too far away for Mahkah to affect. Sophia would have to handle that, although he was uncertain how the young dragonrider would do it. Still, that wasn't his assignment.

Taking a risk he hoped paid off, Mahkah landed Tala in front of the aircraft gearing up for takeoff, earning curious expressions from their pilots.

Standing in front of a bunch of magitech jets wasn't a move anyone expected. They also didn't know what was coming next or that there was no escaping it.

Letting out a carefree scream, Evan held his hands above his head as Coral sailed past the ground transports. She flicked her tail back and forth, intentionally knocking into the jeeps and semi-trucks, hoping to enrage the drivers.

The vehicles teetered to one side and then the other before landing back on their wheels.

Evan could have had Coral knock them over completely, but where would the fun be in that? This was a game of cat and mouse for him.

The first step was to get them to follow. Evan turned his dragon around and headed for the water in the distance that surrounded the base. It was probably to help with perimeter control, but in this instance, it was hopefully going to take down the vehicles confined to the ground.

Evan turned to look over his shoulder, a smile unfurling on his face.

He knew how to antagonize, and in this case, it had worked.

The vehicles were following.

Take down a 747, Sophia said to Lunis.

No, problem, he replied. *I don't think I can in this current form, but if we go after them now, we get it before it takes off.*

And what then? she questioned. *You're going to chew its tires off so it can't get off the ground?*

You realize I'm not a Labrador, right? he fired back.

As awesome as you are in your current form, there's not a hell of a lot of damage we can do, even with how badass you are, she replied.

So I have to shift, he stated.

And by that time, the 747 will be in the air.

Not a problem, Lunis asserted with confidence. *Just get ready for a seat change. The saddle you're in is about to come unglued.*

CHAPTER FIFTY-SIX

Watching his riders spring into action was by far the most thrilling thing Hiker Wallace had seen in a hundred years. No, two hundred. No, in all his life.

He had led many a battle. He had been at the center of some of the most important fights that changed history. That had saved countries. And yet, watching four lone riders move into position to take down magitech that outnumbered them was exhilarating. It was also terrifying.

He knew Mahkah had experience, and that would aid the rider as he took down the ground transports. Wilder was the bravest of his riders, and he had no doubt he could handle the aircraft. Evan? Well, he was the loose cannon, and Hiker could only hope his first real battle wouldn't be his last.

Then there was Sophia Beaufont. She was a surprise at every turn, doing things he never expected.

Hiker wasn't sure why he'd assigned her to the 747. It was what was left to be assigned, and she was the wild card—the one who used strategy over power.

If anything brought down that plane, it would be Sophia Beaufont and Lunis.

He believed that, but only half-heartedly, which was why when the blue dragon transformed with the moon at his back, Hiker thought he was hallucinating.

"Oh, angels above," he gasped, grabbing his beard as his eyes widened in astonishment.

"For the love of all that's holy," Wilder yelled, his lungs emptying of air as he watched Lunis transform in the distance.

He knew little about Sophia Beaufont and her dragon, and now he saw that they had kept the best secret at bay.

"Rock on, you amazing woman," Wilder said as the jets released their first round at him and Simi. "Now it's my turn to be badass."

Mahkah had suspected what Lunis' gift would be, but watching something like that before his very eyes went beyond magic. It spoke of the greatness that was Sophia and her dragon.

Dragons were controlled by elements, which was amazing in itself. That meant that like Hiker, they were stronger in the sun. Or like Thad, that fire fueled them. All of them had a unique advantage, but doing what Lunis had just done was the stuff of legends.

It was the kind of thing that in Mahkah's long life made this moment, in the midst of thousands of others, stand out.

He could live the rest of his life seeing only the spectacular, and he would never see anything like what he just witnessed.

"Woot! Woot!" Evan cheered as he watched Lunis transform from a medium-sized dragon the size of a small recreational vehicle into something as large as the plane he was going after.

He'd first seen this stunt when they were rescuing the dragon eggs, and it had been thrilling to witness then. Watching the other riders react was much more entertaining.

CHAPTER FIFTY-SEVEN

The missiles raced toward Wilder, unrelenting as they targeted him and his dragon.

He yawned, pretending the whole affair was boring him to death. When the missiles were fifty yards away, he simply waved his hand as if shooing away a fly.

And just like that, the winds changed direction in front of him, sweeping the weapons back around and turning on those who had launched them.

The expressions on the pilots' faces as they realized their attacks were quickly rushing back in their direction was intoxicating.

Wilder cheered as the wind did his bidding.

The hum of the motors racing toward Mahkah was enough to make him want to take flight on Tala. He was not accustomed to this world and its technology. It would take time for him to wrap his mind around how things worked now.

And yet, he stayed frozen in place as the menacing vehicles

raced in his direction, ready to take flight, their weapons at the ready.

Mahkah waited until they were close, knowing this would only work if he timed it absolutely right. Unfortunately for him and Tala, the planes' projectiles had a much greater range than his.

Shots were fired at him, and they were forced to take flight to avoid a collision. Darting away from attacks became his focus as Tala soared back and forth.

We must get back on the ground, he urged his dragon.

And we will, she promised, diving for the dusty Earth below. It was both a risky place to be and the only one where they stood a chance of defeating their enemy.

"This is how we play," Evan said, sending Coral into the air as the vehicles progressed in his direction, having taken the bait.

A tank lowered its gun, pointing it at them. The jeep, stocked with its own weapons, roared as it approached.

They were close, but not quite close enough.

Evan had to do another lap, hoping to get the guys with the big guns to continue to pursue.

However, his luck had run out, and soon the shots started, raining all around him and making Coral divert off course to avoid being struck. Several blasts bypassed her wings, nearly scorching them.

They circled back around, diving close to the largest basin of water that surrounded the perimeter.

The tank and jeeps were close now. Almost close enough.

Evan had one chance. After that, his secret would be out. That was why Coral hovered just over the surface of the water, enticing their enemy as he cackled, a sound that always encouraged others to play with him.

He hoped it worked this time.

The saddle had broken off Lunis and fallen to the Earth below. Sophia now stood on her dragon's back, her sword in one hand and her other hand out for balance.

Lunis' transformation to his larger size had taken time. They'd lost the advantage on the 747, and it had taken flight, but Lunis was now faster than usual and quickly gained on the plane. Soon it would be outside the barrier, but not by much.

Somehow, someway they had to ground that plane before it got close to the city. Not only did they not know what was on board, but they also couldn't risk damaging it in case it was highly explosive.

CHAPTER FIFTY-EIGHT

The attacks sent to knock out Wilder connected with the jets after they had been launched. The planes exploded, great balls of fire that lit the sky and rained back down on the tarmac, creating more explosions around the facility.

Many landed on other vehicles, and huge sparks shot up as the domino effect continued.

Wilder darted around new attacks sent by jets that had taken off after the others. They had obviously missed the first show.

He and Simi had one more in them. That was it, and then they'd be done with the wind.

Wilder circled around, grateful for the ease with which Simi soared, her excitement to twirl around attacks and through plumes of smoke thrilling.

For their first battle, this was one for the memory book. He glanced toward where Sophia and Lunis were quickly racing after a huge plane. Somehow, he felt none of this would have happened if not for the girl riding the giant dragon.

Mahkah and Tala landed with a heavy thud, far less graceful than usual. What followed was of much more concern for the aircraft preparing to take off. The ground rumbled under their feet, but Tala didn't move.

Even when the Earth split under the dragon's feet, she didn't move. Instead, her eyes flashed red as a crack shot in the direction of the magitech planes, making them falter toward the ravine that was quickly opening and sending them sliding sideways.

Some spilled straight into the canyon, falling toward the middle of the Earth. Others simply toppled to the side, losing their precious balance.

"That's the thing about us all," Mahkah said in a hushed voice, mostly to himself. "We stand upright until something more powerful knocks us over."

When the ground vehicles were almost at the water's edge, Evan flew over them before spinning around and racing back toward the water. He needed to be on the other side of it if he didn't want to be taken down by his dragon's attack. However, they were firing now, and that was changing the whole flow of his fight.

"Hey, stay off the hair," he said, ducking and covering his head as something whizzed by his head.

He didn't know what all these fancy machines did or shot, only that they needed to be taken down.

Twice he and Coral had to swerve to avoid becoming casualties. To both their relief, they made it over the water before they were pulverized.

Maybe the men in the vehicles thought they'd retreated to safety. Maybe they thought they'd given up. The heavy smoke in the air from the various other fights made it hard to see everything.

Evan noticed the vehicles starting to retreat, which wouldn't work for this attack at all. He encouraged Coral to open her mouth and send them a message to make them back up.

The dragon sent a huge plume of fire at the tanks and jeeps. It blasted over the tops of their windshields, which were apparently fireproof. The important thing was, it made them pause.

"Oh, did you all get a burnie?" Evan called to his enemies. "No problem. We'll cool you off with some water."

He raised his hands, and following the movement, a huge wave of water rose out of the basin in front of them, coming up for fifty yards on either side. The wall rose up until it was even with the dragon and rider hovering above the surface, also fifty yards up. And then, like starting a race, Evan dropped his arms, and the water fell too, crashing to the ground and flooding the vehicles threatening to take them down.

How do we take it down? Sophia asked as they raced after the 747.

Magic, Lunis answered.

She shook her head. *We can't use fire or deadly force. We need to ground that sucker, but the only way I can think of is to gently encourage it back down.*

Well, the good thing is that I'm a big cuddly bear, Lunis said, spreading out his giant arms as he shot forward, moving so fast it made Sophia's teeth hurt. Still, she wasn't deterred by the blast of cold wind that made her eyes water. She didn't feel like she needed to be strapped in as they zoomed miles over the Earth's surface. She was anchored to Lunis like she was a part of him—and in all honesty, she was.

They quickly gained on the 747 and took a higher position. Several times it tried to change course, but it was unable to outmaneuver them. Lunis was too fast and his movements were too stealthy.

When he overtook the plane, soaring overhead, the pilots had to know they were out of options.

Even if it was fueled by the strongest magitech known to man or woman, there was nothing that could hold it up when the next maneuver hit it.

Gently, Lunis lowered his front feet and placed them on the wings of the plane, lowering his body weight onto the aircraft. His back legs found the back end of the plane, and his claws hooked into place.

The engines sputtered, failing under the huge new burden. The pilots had no choice but to make an emergency landing. To Sophia's great relief, it was going to be just inside the borders of the facility, on the flooded ground where another takeoff would be unlikely.

CHAPTER FIFTY-NINE

The Dragon Elite landed one by one around their leader on the roof of the skyscraper in the center of the base. Around them, devastation ensued. The base was flooding, thanks to Evan. A huge fault line had created a crack that split buildings, overturned planes, and created fires that were spreading. The winds Wilder had used to boomerang attacks had added to the destruction, and now the things they'd done were dominoing, quickly creating more damage as one thing started another.

The 747 was back on the ground, and with it, whatever it was carrying.

Sophia landed next to Hiker, her eyes on him as he stared at something in the distance.

"Good work," he said softly, knowing all his riders could hear him.

None of them answered as he urged his dragon toward the edge of the building.

Something was approaching, something that wasn't a jet plane or a helicopter or anything else they'd so far encountered.

For some reason, Sophia believed it was time for her and the guys to stand down. What came next was Hiker's battle.

As if sensing her thoughts, Hiker turned back and looked at his men and Sophia and drew a breath. "I trust you'll have my back, but hopefully, you won't need to. What comes next is Thad."

They all nodded at their leader, but their attention was stolen by what rose over the side of the skyscraper. It was unlike anything Sophia had ever seen or even conceived.

It was incredible in design. It was alive and also not. It was horribly wrong and also ingenious. And most importantly, it was possibly going to be the end of the Dragon Elite.

CHAPTER SIXTY

A dragon with Thad Reinhart on its back rose into view above the skyscraper on top of which they all stood, but this was unlike any dragon Sophia had ever seen.

It was unlike any dragon ever.

Ember, Thad's dragon, wasn't dead. That much was clear now.

The dragon Thad Reinhart rode was half-real, her orange body reflecting the fires and lights all around them. But where one of her wings flapped normally, the other made a crunching noise as the machinery worked to keep her aloft. One of her red eyes was real, and the other was a bulb that shone like a headlight. The dragon was an amalgamation of blood and vessels and mechanics.

Ember was the first cyborg dragon. She was magnificent, and also wrong in every way possible.

Dragons were meant to be magic. They were meant for the ethereal.

This dragon was nothing like where she came from.

That was evident in the way all the other dragons on the rooftop tensed.

"Hiker!" Thad yelled from atop his cyborg dragon, his scarred face making his mouth move strangely. "You found me."

Sophia saw Hiker's back tense as he tightened his hands on the reins. "Ember didn't die?" Astonishment overflowed in his tone. Thad had wanted this reveal, and evidenced by the laugh he let out, he'd gotten the reaction he'd been going for.

"Oh, no," Thad replied. "You thought Adam ended her. I thought so too, but I'm a fighter. You've been given everything your whole life, but I've fought for it, and I found a way to bring back my girl." He carefully stroked the dragon's face, which was mostly metal.

"How?" Hiker growled, running his eyes over the impossible beast hovering before them.

"Magitech, of course," Thad answered. "But more importantly, I used dragons. Why do you think they are almost extinct?"

"No!" Hiker yelled.

"Oh, yes," Thad replied, pleased with himself.

"How could you do this?" Hiker asked. "You know better than anyone how important dragons are, no matter what side you align with."

Thad shook his head. "You've always forgotten I have no side." He threw his hand out at his facility, which was full of chaos, fire, and water everywhere. "I don't even care that you've destroyed something I've worked so hard for. I'll build it again after I finish you and your riders. Should I take you all at once or one at a time? Either way, there's no getting away this time, Hiker. Ainsley isn't here to save you."

Sophia felt Wilder turn and look at her. He knew now. They all did. It would be hard for Hiker to hide the truth now, but that was the least of his worries. He had to survive this, and there was nothing Sophia could do to help.

The stage was set, and Hiker Wallace was the only warrior from the Dragon Elite allowed on it.

CHAPTER SIXTY-ONE

Bell's form seemed to grow as the dragon rushed forward to spring off the edge of the building. She flew toward the enemy.

Thad didn't take it easy on them, immediately firing the guns laced into Ember's wings.

Hiker ducked as the shots whizzed past them, bullets spraying everywhere, making the dragons on the rooftop scatter. Lunis rolled over, pinning Sophia to the surface. Thankfully he'd returned to his normal size and tented himself over her, deflecting the bullets with his tough hide.

Those bullets were meant to take out a human, not a dragon. That worried Sophia, and she pushed up from the ground, urging Lunis off her.

When she could see before her again, her heart leapt. Things weren't going well for Hiker. He was losing before the battle had even started.

One of Bell's wings had been hit, and she was favoring it as she tried to stay up. Hiker had his sword out and brandished it as his brother, who was higher in the air and looking down at him, laughing.

"You never got it, Hiker," Thad yelled down to him. "Good does not win. It never has."

"You're wrong!" Hiker screamed, a guttural ache in his voice.

"I'm not," Thad said in a low voice all of them could hear.

The leader of the Dragon Elite was one attack away from defeat. That much was obvious to all that were watching. And yet, the riders couldn't intervene. They simply watched as Hiker struggled to stay upright and Bell hurt. Any attacks they made were going to be hard to place. Bell was trying to make up the lost space, continuing to flap her wings.

"The thing about you, Hiker," Thad went on, "is that you were always meant to lose. You don't have what it takes. You never did, and now you'll lose with everyone watching, as you were meant to from the beginning. Goodbye, brother."

The cyborg dragon shot a blast at Hiker Wallace none of them could have averted, and it hit him in the chest. It knocked Bell over, making her roll head over feet.

The lucky part for the dragon and rider was they crashed on the roof of the skyscraper, where they tumbled one on top of the other until they were completely still.

CHAPTER SIXTY-TWO

"Noooooo!" Sophia yelled, sliding off Lunis and trying to race forward. Wilder caught her arm and pulled her back.

"No," he whispered. "He's not out just yet. Have hope."

"But he is," she wailed, watching as Hiker Wallace, bloody and mostly broken, pushed up from his dragon, who was trying to fold her wing back.

The leader of the Dragon Elite staggered toward the edge of the building. Sophia worried he was so disoriented he'd simply walk over the side. Instead, he halted a few feet from the edge.

"Is this what you wanted?" Hiker held a finger out to his brother.

Thad laughed. "Of course. And now for the finishing blow."

He turned his cyborg dragon around like she was a piece of machinery. Sophia could have sworn she heard the dragon beeping as it backed up, like a pickup truck. Her imagination was taking over, trying to block out the events she was seeing. None of it seemed real. None of it seemed right. Good guys were supposed to win. The bad were supposed to fall. That's how it had to go.

"We have to help him!" Sophia yelled, trying to jerk out of Wilder's grasp.

He held her tight, not letting her go. "No, Soph. He has to do this on his own."

"If he doesn't, he will die," she whispered back. "Don't let him die."

"Soph, there's nothing to do."

They both looked up as the gun under Ember's magitech wing glowed, charging up to fire. It was aimed straight at Hiker, and it would end him. He was too disoriented, staggering around and trying to find his footing, to dodge anything. Bell was in no shape to fight either. Her wings were badly injured, and her body burned. Whatever had hit her wasn't something she would easily recover from.

Sophia felt into her pocket for the frequency disk. She brought her chin up, conviction in her eyes. "There's always something we can do to save those who matter. Please, Wild. Let me go."

She knew, and so did Wilder, that if he didn't let her go, she'd stay pinned. Sophia was the master of strategy, not strength.

He saw something in her that caused him to release her. His hands let up on her shoulders. He seemed torn, but he allowed her to pull away. "I hope you know what you're doing."

"I don't," she said to him as she backed away. "I never do, though. It's all instinct."

She turned and raced toward the only leader she'd ever known. The only one she'd wanted to follow. She wasn't letting Hiker go without a fight—even if he hated her for it.

CHAPTER SIXTY-THREE

Before Thad Reinhart noticed her, Sophia ducked into the shadows of the rooftop, cast by Bell, who had crouched in her agony. She'd do anything to take the pain from the dragon, but there were more pressing matters to attend to.

Sophia rolled and dove until she was crouched just behind Hiker.

"What was that?" Thad asked, his voice barely audible over the hum of the guns about to deliver a five-hundred-year-old man's untimely death.

"Just a pain in the ass," Hiker answered, his eyes diving to the side as he glanced over his shoulder, seeing Sophia.

Thad apparently didn't think much of this reply. He simply grunted as his attention stayed focused on the guns charging.

Sophia didn't waste any time activating the frequency disk. The red meter started to build. She hoped it wasn't too late, and Ember's software hadn't figured out how to troubleshoot it after the first attempt.

The large man continued to sway in front of her. Sophia was afraid Hiker would tumble over the side of the building before she could help him. She used the last thing she had remaining—her words.

"Sir," she said in a whisper only he could hear, the roar of the charging gun too loud for Thad.

Hiker tensed and listened.

"You are better than him. You are stronger. And we have your back."

She glanced down to find the red meter all the way to the top. The device was ready.

"Now it's time for you to have your front," she said, looking back and finding Hiker Wallace's sword lying next to his injured dragon. She grabbed it just as the humming of the gun ceased.

"What?" Thad yelled as his dragon descended, losing elevation.

"Sir!" Sophia yelled, thrusting the sword into the air.

Hiker spun and grabbed it in a fluid motion that nearly stole her heart. He still had his grace, even injured. His speed and strength followed with a flash of perseverance in his eyes. Hiker Wallace wasn't done yet.

The frequency disk had taken effect. Fear flashed in Ember's eyes. It quickly spread to Thad Reinhart—panic taking over both dragon and rider.

The lights on the dragon dimmed. The humming dissipated. It's wings froze.

"What have you done?" Thad yelled, frantically searching his dragon for the cause of the problem.

The cyborg dragon was quickly losing height and beginning to spiral, her wings folding in, bringing her closer to the edge of the building. With Thad on her back, his face full of terror, Ember fell toward the skyscraper.

Her wing folded in, crushing into the roof as she dove face first into the hard surface. Ember teetered halfway on the edge of the building. Her rider was forced to the side, hanging mostly off. Thad's attention was on Ember. He was scrambling, trying to figure out how to keep her from falling over the side, plummeting to what would be certain death this time.

Hiker didn't hesitate. This time when his brother fell toward him, he brought his sword around and down, decisively ending the one man who had terrorized him since the beginning.

The scream that cut through the night air was full of pain and regret. Thad's face contorted with terror as Hiker shoved the sword deeper through his brother's abdomen, pinning him straight down to the surface of the roof, making his head hit the concrete hard. The man's hands reached for Hiker, but he was powerless to stop his twin from twisting the sword, making the wound even deadlier.

Hiker then picked up his boot and with a deliberate shove, he kicked at the side of the dragon, sending her out from beside Thad. The metal scraped the rooftop but it didn't stop the dragon that was dangerously teetering over the side. Nothing Ember could do would stop her from what happened next. And she seemed mostly paralyzed without magitech. Much like her rider, she was powerless. Thad was pinned to the roof as Ember was sent with a brute force across the distance.

The dragon's body slid over the edge and down the side of the building. Thad, seeming more dead than alive, reached longingly for his dragon, but she was gone. And soon he would be too as he stayed stuck to the rooftop by a single blade—blood everywhere.

Hiker Wallace stood on the roof, his breathing heavy and his balance wavering as he looked down at his brother, watching him take his final breath. Hiker didn't appear victorious as his enemy perished but he was alive, and the greatest battle of his life was over.

CHAPTER SIXTY-FOUR

The cold of the Gullington air was the most welcome thing Sophia had ever felt. She didn't remember the hands that pulled her through the portal.

She didn't remember how they got there. All she knew was that she and Lunis had at the last moment sent all their magical energy to Hiker Wallace to keep him from tumbling over the edge of the building when he was at his weakest, right after the death of his twin brother. He actually tumbled forward, but she had stopped it. Lunis had helped.

Now the bigger question was who had saved her. Brought her back.

She didn't know.

But somehow, she was staring at the leader of the Dragon Elite on the frozen ground of the Gullington, not wishing to be anywhere but Scotland.

CHAPTER SIXTY-FIVE

The next morning brought a headache unlike any Sophia had ever experienced. With it came the realization that the world was brand new.

She awoke in her bed in the Gullington, soft and comforting, with so many questions.

Sophia sat bolt upright to find Ainsley smiling at her.

"You did it, S. Beaufont," the housekeeper said.

"Do you mean, I saved Hiker Wallace?" she asked, curious.

The shapeshifter shook her head. "Oh, no. He's madder than hell. In five hundred years, I've never seen him this angry. I was saying you finally got the men to behave."

Sophia swung her feet over the side of the bed, confused. "Ains? What do you mean?"

The mischievous housekeeper had her robe at the ready and held it out for her. "Find out for yourself, S. Beaufont."

Sophia stood, her feet faltering under her from tiredness unlike any she'd ever known. She slid her arms into the robe and shrugged it onto her shoulders.

The housekeeper led her out of her room, making her press her eyes shut like it was a strange birthday party, although Sophia had been born in the summer, not the winter. Spring would be dawning soon, she realized.

With a care that made Sophia's heart tighten, Ainsley led her down the steps to the foyer. When Sophia was at the bottom, the housekeeper said, "Open up."

Sophia Beaufont opened her eyes to find something she'd never imagined.

CHAPTER SIXTY-SIX

Standing before Sophia Beaufont, the first female dragonrider in the Dragon Elite, were four polished men, ready to impress.

They were the sight she hadn't seen when she'd first entered the Castle, and they were every bit as perfect.

Sophia loved them for everything they were and everything they were trying to be to impress her.

She stood looking ridiculous in her pajamas and glared at Evan, Mahkah, Wilder, and Hiker as they nudged each other to stand straighter, look better, be more polished.

"Hey," she said to the four men before her.

"Hey," they all said in unison, sounding like a bunch of bumbling idiots, although she had to admit they didn't look like it.

Evan looked nice in his black suit. Regal, almost.

Mahkah was sophisticated, which matched his demeanor.

And Wilder? Well, he was more than nice, but more on that later.

As for Hiker, he was alive. For Sophia, that was all that mattered.

She went straight to the leader of the Dragon Elite with a wide grin on her face. "You made it," she said, knowing better than to offer a hug.

He shook his head as if she had offered such a thing. "I told you not to help me."

"Deal with it, old man," she retorted.

He lowered his chin, offering her kind eyes. "I wouldn't be here if not for you. It wasn't anything short of sacrifice that saved me, and it was you.

"I just didn't want Evan to be our leader," she answered with a laugh.

"Dude," Evan called, "I can hear you."

Hiker grabbed her hand and pulled her off to the side. "I can't thank you enough. There is little that divides us from life and death, I've found. It's usually just a well-placed friend. Thanks for being mine."

"Anytime, sir."

CHAPTER SIXTY-SEVEN

Spring was coming; Sophia could feel it. Somehow a warm breeze had appeared, and she had grown accustomed to it during her recent journeys.

She stood on the Expanse, feeling the breeze on her back. She was glad Thad was dead and the wars he'd started were over. She knew more battles were waiting to be waged. And then there was the end of dragonriders.

No one was ready to deal with that. Sophia knew she had to move on.

Sophia took one step toward the Pond and then another.

Each seemed to lead somewhere, although she wasn't sure why. She didn't even know where she was going when her feet led her to the other side of the Castle. It was where the Expanse met the Pond, which was a strange place to find oneself. But here she was, with an ache in her heart and the blue of the water spreading before her.

And then she saw what she had been looking for without knowing it.

Quiet.

The gnome poked his head out of a cave and withdrew it again.

She thought about ignoring him, but then he looked out again and glanced straight at her, and his eyes connected with her as he said, "Hey, you!"

Sophia's feet carried her to him.

CHAPTER SIXTY-EIGHT

The door to the cave was mostly closed.

Sophia held her breath, not understanding why her heart was beating rapidly, or why she felt like she was on the edge of something great.

She was just catching Quiet in an act of mischief.

When she pulled back the great stone door to this mysterious cave, she got it.

Sophia knew, and then she didn't. She soaked it all in, disbelieving, before she ran for the Castle, fetching Mom and Dad. Or in this case, Mama Jamba and Hiker Wallace, the only parents the girl had ever known.

CHAPTER SIXTY-NINE

Hiker Wallace slowed before they entered the cave as if he knew what they'd see, but he didn't. There was no way.

He covered his mouth. "Soph, what is this? What do you need to show me?"

She retreated back into the cave, waving him forward and encouraging him to follow. "I don't know, sir. I mean, not entirely, but I'm sure we'll get an explanation."

He hadn't said much about the rescue, not really. What he hadn't said was still evident in his eyes, and now he seemed reluctant in a different way. He was whole and broken at the same time. Hiker Wallace had finished his brother, the biggest threat he'd ever known, yet that was accompanied by the idea that his kind—the dragonriders—were done.

"Just trust me, sir," she said, sidling up to the cave door she'd just found. Before she could finish her sentence, she saw Quiet in the distance, and for some reason, she knew there was nothing else to say.

All questions were gone as she pushed open the cave door.

Hiker Wallace's awe was equal to hers and he gasped.

CHAPTER SEVENTY

One thousand dragon eggs, full of potential, sparkled at Hiker Wallace and Sophia Beaufont as they entered the cave curated by the great Quiet, the groundskeeper for the Gullington.

They gaped at a sight most would never see.

"How?" Hiker asked after a long moment.

"Because," Mama Jamba answered from a distant corner where no one expected her to be standing, "she's Sophia Beaufont, and she completed her training."

"What?" Sophia asked since that was the only question in her mind.

"My dear, haven't you wondered what Quiet has been doing?" Mama Jamba asked.

"Every day," Sophia answered.

"He's been starting the seeds of sacred new beginnings," Mama Jamba stated, kneeling and cupping an egg.

"I don't understand," Sophia argued. "I thought the eggs were all gone."

"They were," Mama Jamba explained. "But that was from the first rider. There were always supposed to be two."

"Her?" Hiker asked, pointing at Sophia and looking around, perplexed.

"That's right," Mama answered. "The first rider came about when the first and only dragon landed on Earth. An experiment of sorts. That union with the first male rider spawned one thousand eggs—the first set. Then I decided, with the angels, that we'd have more riders, but I had no idea how to have more until now. It was Sophia who spawned the idea and this batch of one thousand eggs."

"If the first male rider got one thousand eggs..." Sophia said to herself.

"Then the first female also gets a thousand," Mama Jamba agreed. Mother Nature cupped her hands. "This is my gift to you —your eggs. Know that some will be good, and some will be bad. They are yours and not yours. That's how it works when you're a mother. You own your children, but you don't."

Sophia nodded obediently, looking at Hiker for direction. He was still the leader of the Dragon Elite, and that was how it was meant to be for as long as time, as far as she was concerned.

Finally, Sophia looked at Mother Nature and smiled with gratitude. "I promise to take care of them for all time, Mama."

She patted her side. "I think they will take care of you, but whatever, my love."

CHAPTER SEVENTY-ONE

The atmosphere in the Castle was different when Sophia returned after discovering the eggs. Hiker admitted to telling the guys about them.

But there was something else to it.

There was potential pouring up from the creaks in the floor, Sophia felt. She also had the distinct impression she was being watched. She glanced around the entrance hall, feeling strangely disoriented from the weight of everything.

She wasn't sure why but she turned to find Quiet smiling at her in a way she couldn't explain. The gnome stood in the shadows with a glint in his eyes.

She thought he might murder her or crown her at any moment with the strange looks he was giving her.

Sophia wanted to ask him about the eggs. Thank him. But then an arm hooked around her shoulder and she was swept away, her attention stolen.

"The thing about Quiet is," Wilder began steering her in the direction of the Valentine's Day feast, "he has a crush on you because you've been leading him on."

Sophia slapped him. "I have not."

"Well, of course, you have," Wilder argued. "You are available, we have no one like you, and you're all batting your eyelashes at him."

"There's no way to look at him without batting my eyelashes," Sophia argued.

He nodded. "Thanks for taking my literal point. You're good at that."

She shook her head, deciding to abandon talking to commoners like Wilder. That brought her to talking to Mama Jamba, who gave her a considering look as she approached.

"So, you knew about the eggs?" Sophia asked, taking a bite of a heart-shaped cookie. "That was the business with the training, wasn't it?"

"Oh, my dear, you don't think you've figured me out by now?" Mama Jamba asked coyly.

"No, I wouldn't dream of it," Sophia answered.

"Anyway, so you're happy here? At the Gullington?" Mama Jamba asked, grabbing Sophia's hands and holding them tight with great intent. "That's the biggest question, and the only one I can't answer for you."

Sophia didn't know how to answer for a moment, feeling a strange draw toward Mother Nature rather than the Castle. Then she decided it didn't matter. It was all the same.

"I'm more than happy. This is my forever home," Sophia finally answered.

Her thoughts ran over her like a waterfall. These people were her family. Her chosen family. Evan might annoy her. Quiet intrigued. Mahkah was an enigma. No one made her laugh like Wilder. And then there was Ainsley, who she needed to help, although she wasn't sure why or if it would matter. There was no one she respected more than Hiker. These people, all the Dragon Elite had left, were her family.

Familia est Sempiternum.

One day, the family would grow. The thousand dragon eggs

nestled in the cave by the Pond guaranteed that. There would be more dragons one day, and with that would come the potential of new riders.

The Dragon Elite weren't done. Not by a long shot.

In a way, they were just getting started.

Sophia looked around the dining hall, smiling as everyone cheered, grateful for the celebration.

These people at the Gullington were all her family.

And Sophia Beaufont was going to do whatever was needed to protect them all from now on.

SARAH'S AUTHOR NOTES

Thank you so much for reading. Your support of the Liv Beaufont series and this one has been life changing. Thank you! Seriously! Thank you.

Right before writing this book, I went and spent a week in
Scotland. I'd been wanting to so since the 20Booksto50K conference in Edinburgh. However, I had a series of life complications
that prevented that from happening. My cat was mauled by a
coyote. My daughter needed me home. And I needed to be there.
So I didn't go and I thought that was okay. But the desire to see
Scotland never left me...

And then I wrote a bunch of books. And then I had to keep a
child alive. And then I went to Vegas for the main conference.
And I got back and was like, damn it, I'm going to Scotland.

Here's the truth. I was burned out. I'd written 15 Liv and
Sophia books in one year. I love those gals. They are Lydia, my
daughter, and me. But writing nonstop is draining. I don't usually
go out on the weekends I don't have my daughter. I wake up, go
to Pilates, put back on my pajamas and then write for 12 hours.
And then repeat.

So when I got back from Vegas and couldn't shake Scotland from my mind, the location for the Gullington, I didn't let it go. I did something I've never done and booked a spontaneous trip. I didn't really know anyone there. J.L. Hendricks was hanging there. RE Vance and lives there. But I didn't have a travel companion which is weird for me. I've never traveled alone internationally.

And it was incredible. It was a soulful trip where I learned how to be alone and make friends and realize I'm never alone no matter where I am.

I worried I wouldn't have anyone to eat with. That I wouldn't be able to navigate the city. That I'd be lonely. None of those things happened.

And I learned so much about Scotland which I hoped made this book richer for you. I hiked to the top of Arthur's Seat and pretended I was Sophia Beaufont. The skies were blue and the sun clearly shining. The Scotsman who led the way told me that it's rare to have a day like that in December in Edinburgh, but he's never been on that hike with a Cali girl.

When we got to the top the winds were so fierce he said he'd never experienced that in Scotland. Again, he'd never been with an LA girl—we make things happen (or at least I do). So there we were, on the top of a peak, the winds blowing our hair back and the sun shining. Talk about inspiration! We watched a storm move in, blowing across the North Sea. These are the things that fuel stories.

I pretended I was S. Beaufont riding on Lunis. The winds were so intense, the puddles had a current. The Scotsman, with a prideful look, told me about how the wind makes them stronger. They brace their shoulders and charge into it. You know that went into the book.

I found the Scots to be such sweet and lovely people. I got back saying, "Thank you. That's lovely. Cheers." I also took so much inspiration from the trip. This book is littered with things from that trip.

I can't tell you how much that trip refilled my inspirational vault. As writers we are constantly putting out creative stuff into the world, but it's important that we remember to refill our reserves. I soaked it all in. I fell in love with a country. I fell for the people. And I came home with stories unlike I ever thought I'd tell.

I was fortunate enough to make a friend with a native Scotsman and he taught me a lot. That's how I was able to discuss things like the Scots New Year in this book and their vernacular. I came back saying "quite" and "wee" a lot and also missing Edinburgh like crazy. I bought him a fork for Christmas. He bought me a gift card. We aren't Wilder and Sophia but we are entertaining nonetheless.

I always want to come home after a trip. Always. And yet, I felt like I left part of my heart in Scotland. Not entirely because of the people (although there was that). Because there had been something calling me there since before I started this series. And now it calls me back.

But I have so many places that demand my attention. I have so many stories to tell. So who knows if I'll go back. Only time.

Currently, I'm on a plane to Montana for a family reunion…in freaking January. Wish me luck. I hope not to freeze. Expect to see Sophia in the artic with Lunis. Lydia is so excited to see snow. I'm excited to take a break from the books because when I return, my focus is better. I love my characters and miss them when we take time apart, but we are richer for the break.

I love to travel. I love staying home and writing books you all enjoy. And more than anything, I love doing it with people I enjoy. Thanks MA for being awesome. Here's to another year of creating addictive stories together.

Now, it's his turn to tell you all about how I blamed him for the trip to Scotland to anyone who would listen. It couldn't be my idea so I told everyone that he "made" me do it.

Drops the mic and walks away.

(Written January 25, 2019)

MICHAEL'S AUTHOR NOTES

You know, TinyNinja™, as an adult you start to learn how to accept the blame of your choices, or the CREDIT when you do something fantastic.

You went to Scotland by yourself… that is pretty fantastic. So, I'll pick the mic up and give it back to you.

While you and I don't talk very much,Sarah - except on books and beats and covers - you have my admiration for what you have accomplished with Liv Beaufont and now S. Beaufont. Two sisters who are changing lives, not just those in the stories, but for you and her daughter.

Oh, and for those living in Scotland as you market their country to readers around the world.

(Truly, Edinburgh is a wonderful city and it deserves all of the attention we can give it. Not for Edinburgh, but rather in case we help a few readers decide to look into traveling to Scotland – it does fill up a soul quite well. And empty your pocketbook.

That might or might not be a comment on the prices or the fact their beer is plentiful. I'm not admitting which.)

Ad Aeternitatem,

Michael Anderle

(Written January 27, 2019)

ACKNOWLEDGMENTS

SARAH NOFFKE

I feel like I'm on the stage at the Oscars, accepting an award when I write my acknowledgments. I stand there, holding this award, my hands shaking and my words racing around in my mind. I'm not an actress for a reason. I'm a writer and talking to people in "real life" is hard. Not to mention a ton of people all at once.

I picture looking out at the audience and being blinded by spotlights and forgetting every word of the speech I memorized just in case I won. The speech would go like this and it's meant for all of you, not the guild. For the fans. The supporters. The people who are the reason I would ever stand on any stage, ever.

Okay, here we go. I clear my throat and smile, looking up at the camera, holding the little golden man. And then I begin:

This was never supposed to happen. I was never meant to publish a book and then another one. And then another. I was supposed to write in private and live a life that Henry David Thoreau called a life of "quiet desperation." I would always hope to share my books, but never bring myself to do it. And you would never read my words. But then, in a crazed moment of brashness, I did share my books and you all liked them. And because of that, I've never been the same. And here I am feeling grateful all just because...

That's why I'm here. Because of you. Thank you to my first readers. The ones who picked up those books that I didn't even outline and you still liked them. You messaged me and maybe you thought it was no big deal, but when your ego is new to the publishing world, it's a big deal.

I can't thank you readers enough. I've found that reading your reviews helps me to start a chapter when I'm stuck or lazy.

I really need to thank someone who has made this all possible and that's my father. I was going to quit. I can't tell you how many times I quit. But when I wasn't making it, he was the one who told me to not throw in the towel. "Give yourself a timeline," he suggested. If I didn't get to my goal by then, I'd quit. And apparently there was magic in that advice, because I'm still doing this. Dad, you're the pragmatic one, but when you believed in me enough to tell me to not quit, I knew I had to follow your advice.

And I thank all my friends who are constantly supporting me with thoughts of love and encouragement. Most don't read my books. I'm sort of self-deprecating, although I'm working on it and will be the first to tell my friends, "My books probably aren't for you." However, every now and then a friend surprises me and says, "I was up all night reading your books." It's always a total shock. But my point is, that even if they didn't read, I still have the best friends ever. Diane, you're my rock. And I love you, even though you will probably not read this.

Thank you to everyone at LMBPN. Those people are like family to me, although I'm not sure if they'll let me sleep on their couch. Well, who am I kidding? They totally will. Big thanks to Steve, Lynne, Mihaela, Kelly, Jen and the entire team. The JIT members are the best.

Huge thank you to the LMBPN Ladies group on Facebook. Micky, you're the best. And that group keeps me sane.

And a giant thank you to the betas for this series. Juergen you are my first reader and friend. Thanks for all the help. And thanks to Martin and Crystal for being some of the best people I know. What would I do without you? A huge thanks to the ARC team. Seriously, if it weren't for you all I might pass out before release day, wondering if anyone will like the book.

And with all my books, my final thank you goes to my lovely muse, Lydia. Oh sweet darling, I write these books for you, but ironically, I couldn't write them without you. You are my inspiration. My sounding board. And the reason that I want to succeed. I love you.

Thank you all! I'm sorry if I forgot anyone. Blame Michael. For no other reason than just because.

BOOKS BY SARAH NOFFKE

Sarah Noffke writes YA and NA science fiction, fantasy, paranormal and urban fantasy. In addition to being an author, she is a mother, podcaster and professor. Noffke holds a Masters of Management and teaches college business/writing courses. Most of her students have no idea that she toils away her hours crafting fictional characters. www.sarahnoffke.com

Check out other work by Sarah author here.

Ghost Squadron:

Formation #1:
   Kill the bad guys. Save the Galaxy. All in a hard day's work.
   After ten years of wandering the outer rim of the galaxy, Eddie Teach is a man without a purpose. He was one of the toughest pilots in the Federation, but now he's just a regular guy, getting into bar fights and making a difference wherever he can. It's not the same as flying a ship and saving colonies, but it'll have to do.

That is, until General Lance Reynolds tracks Eddie down and offers him a job. There are bad people out there, plotting terrible things, killing innocent people, and destroying entire colonies. **Someone has to stop them.**

Eddie, along with the genetically-enhanced combat pilot Julianna Fregin and her trusty E.I. named Pip, must recruit a diverse team of specialists, both human and alien. They'll need to master their new Q-Ship, one of the most powerful strike ships ever constructed. And finally, they'll have to stop a faceless enemy so powerful, it threatens to destroy the entire Federation.

All in a day's work, right?

Experience this exciting military sci-fi saga and the latest addition to the expanded Kurtherian Gambit Universe. If you're a fan of Mass Effect, Firefly, or Star Wars, you'll love this riveting new space opera.

NOTE: If cursing is a problem, then this might not be for you.
Check out the entire series <u>here.</u>

The Precious Galaxy Series:

Corruption #1

A new evil lurks in the darkness.

After an explosion, the crew of a battlecruiser mysteriously disappears.

Bailey and Lewis, complete strangers, find themselves suddenly onboard the damaged ship. Lewis hasn't worked a case in years, not since the final one broke his spirit and his bank account. The last thing Bailey remembers is preparing to take down a fugitive on Onyx Station.

Mysteries are harder to solve when there's no evidence left behind.

Bailey and Lewis don't know how they got onboard *Ricky Bobby* or why. However, they quickly learn that whatever was responsible for the explosion and disappearance of the crew is still on the ship.

Monsters are real and what this one can do changes everything.

The new team bands together to discover what happened and how to fight the monster lurking in the bottom of the battle-cruiser.

Will they find the missing crew? Or will the monster end them all?

The Soul Stone Mage Series:

House of Enchanted #1:

The Kingdom of Virgo has lived in peace for thousands of years...until now.

The humans from Terran have always been real assholes to the witches of Virgo. Now a silent war is brewing, and the timing couldn't be worse. Princess Azure will soon be crowned queen of the Kingdom of Virgo.

In the Dark Forest a powerful potion-maker has been murdered.

Charmsgood was the only wizard who could stop a deadly virus plaguing Virgo. He also knew about the devastation the people from Terran had done to the forest.

Azure must protect her people. Mend the Dark Forest. Create alliances with savage beasts. No biggie, right?

But on coronation day everything changes. Princess Azure isn't who she thought she was and that's a big freaking problem.

Welcome to The Revelations of Oriceran. Check out the entire series here.

The Lucidites Series:

Awoken, #1:

Around the world humans are hallucinating after sleepless nights.

In a sterile, underground institute the forecasters keep reporting the same events.

And in the backwoods of Texas, a sixteen-year-old girl is about to be caught up in a fierce, ethereal battle.

Meet Roya Stark. She drowns every night in her dreams, spends her hours reading classic literature to avoid her family's ridicule, and is prone to premonitions—which are becoming more frequent. And now her dreams are filled with strangers offering to reveal what she has always wanted to know: Who is she? That's the question that haunts her, and she's about to find out. But will Roya live to regret learning the truth?

Stunned, #2

Revived, #3

The Reverians Series:

Defects, #1:

In the happy, clean community of Austin Valley, everything appears to be perfect. Seventeen-year-old Em Fuller, however, fears something is askew. Em is one of the new generation of Dream Travelers. For some reason, the gods have not seen fit to gift all of them with their expected special abilities. Em is a Defect—one of the unfortunate Dream Travelers not gifted with a psychic power. Desperate to do whatever it takes to earn her gift, she endures painful daily injections along with commands from her overbearing, loveless father. One of the few bright spots in her life is the return of a friend she had thought dead—but with his return comes the knowledge of a shocking, unforgivable truth. The society Em thought was protecting her has actually been betraying her, but she has no idea how to break away from its authority without hurting everyone she loves.

Rebels, #2

Warriors, #3

Vagabond Circus Series:

Suspended, #1:
When a stranger joins the cast of Vagabond Circus—a circus that is run by Dream Travelers and features real magic—mysterious events start happening. The once orderly grounds of the circus become riddled with hidden threats. And the ringmaster realizes not only are his circus and its magic at risk, but also his very life.

Vagabond Circus caters to the skeptics. Without skeptics, it would close its doors. This is because Vagabond Circus runs for two reasons and only two reasons: first and foremost to provide the lost and lonely Dream Travelers a place to be illustrious. And secondly, to show the nonbelievers that there's still magic in the world. If they believe, then they care, and if they care, then they don't destroy. They stop the small abuse that day-by-day breaks down humanity's spirit. If Vagabond Circus makes one skeptic believe in magic, then they halt the cycle, just a little bit. They allow a little more love into this world. That's Dr. Dave Raydon's mission. And that's why this ringmaster recruits. That's why he directs. That's why he puts on a show that makes people question their beliefs. He wants the world to believe in magic once again.

Paralyzed, #2
Released, #3

Ren Series:

Ren: The Man Behind the Monster, #1:
Born with the power to control minds, hypnotize others, and read thoughts, Ren Lewis, is certain of one thing: God made a mistake. No one should be born with so much power. A monster awoke in him the same year he received his gifts. At ten years old.

A prepubescent boy with the ability to control others might merely abuse his powers, but Ren allowed it to corrupt him. And since he can have and do anything he wants, Ren should be happy. However, his journey teaches him that harboring so much power doesn't bring happiness, it steals it. Once this realization sets in, Ren makes up his mind to do the one thing that can bring his tortured soul some peace. He must kill the monster.

Note This book is NA and has strong language, violence and sexual references.

Ren: God's Little Monster, #2
Ren: The Monster Inside the Monster, #3
Ren: The Monster's Adventure, #3.5
Ren: The Monster's Death

Olento Research Series:

Alpha Wolf, #1:

Twelve men went missing.

Six months later they awake from drug-induced stupors to find themselves locked in a lab.

And on the night of a new moon, eleven of those men, possessed by new—and inhuman—powers, break out of their prison and race through the streets of Los Angeles until they disappear one by one into the night.

Olento Research wants its experiments back. Its CEO, Mika Lenna, will tear every city apart until he has his werewolves imprisoned once again. He didn't undertake a huge risk just to lose his would-be assassins.

However, the Lucidite Institute's main mission is to save the world from injustices. Now, it's Adelaide's job to find these mutated men and protect them and society, and fast. Already around the nation, wolflike men are being spotted. Attacks on innocent women are happening. And then, Adelaide realizes what her next step must be: She has to find the alpha wolf first.

Only once she's located him can she stop whoever is behind this experiment to create wild beasts out of human beings.

Lone Wolf, #2
Rabid Wolf, #3
Bad Wolf, #4

CONNECT WITH THE AUTHORS

Connect with Sarah and sign up for her email list here:

http://www.sarahnoffke.com/connect/

Connect with Michael Anderle and sign up for his email list here:

Website: http://lmbpn.com

Email List: http://lmbpn.com/email/

https://www.facebook.com/LMBPNPublishing

https://twitter.com/MichaelAnderle

https://www.instagram.com/lmbpn_publishing/

https://www.bookbub.com/authors/michael-anderle

www.ingramcontent.com/pod-product-compliance
Lightning Source LLC
Chambersburg PA
CBHW020408110726
47899CB00006B/1896